HOW TO MAKE LOVE TO A NEGRO

First UK publication

'Laferrière brilliantly and hilariously sifts through the tired; frigid beliefs that Western culture lays on African-derived males (and everyone else). . . The 117 pages of HOW TO form a heady meditation, a psychic tussle that resonates with the furious stuff in James Baldwin's essays, or Louis Armstrong's smiling trumpet, or Martin Luther King's oratory: black revelation' – Joe Wood, **Village Voice**

'HOW TO MAKE LOVE TO A NEGRO is sexual politics at its best and most literal. There are layers and layers of meaning to be untangled in this novel. . . It is at once humorous, profound, ribald' – Nancy Nantais, **Charlatan**

'There's a ribald high energy here, a go-for-broke chutzpah that makes other Canadian writing seem anaemic and genteel by comparison. . . Laferrière's book crackles and snaps with the profane and profound power of Jack Kerouac, Henry Miller, Eldridge Cleaver, James Baldwin and Charles Bukowski' – James Adams, **Edmonton Journal**

'The book is calculated to offend both blacks and whites, but most readers will forgive the brash writer. No matter how discomfiting his satire, he is always outrageously funny' – Kate Taylor, **Hamilton Spectator**

HOW TO MAKE
LOVE TO A NEGRO

HOW TO MAKE
LOVE TO A NEGRO

DANY LAFERRIÈRE

Translated by David Homel

BLOOMSBURY

First published in Great Britain 1991

Copyright © Dany Laferrière 1987
Translation copyright © David Homel 1987

The moral right of the author has been asserted

Bloomsbury Publishing Ltd, 2 Soho Square, London W1V 5DE

A CIP catalogue record for this book
is available from the British Library

ISBN 0 7475 0847 X

10   9   8   7   6   5   4   3   2   1

Printed and bound in Great Britain by Clays Ltd, St Ives Plc

Le nègre est un meuble

– Napoleonic Code art. 1, 1685

For Roland Désir, sleeping somewhere on this planet

How to Make Love with the Reader ... Slyly

'When my book came out,' Dany Laferrière recalls with bitterness and amazement, 'nobody believed it was written by a black man. They said, Whoever wrote it writes *almost* like a black. Everyone was so sure it was written by a white. A black couldn't write like *that*, they said.'

But the famous photo of Dany sitting in the Carré St-Louis, in his Miller / Bukowski attitude with gym shoes, typewriter and booze-in-a-bag, left the doubters no way out: the Negro of the title was indeed black.

Why did so many readers doubt the narrator's identity, even after he had revealed his true colours? After all, these same readers were acquainted with black writers rising up to take a stand. The names of some of them are mentioned in this novel as icons, some of which are worn out, others still powerful: James Baldwin, Richard Wright, Chester Himes. But what confounded the expectations of Laferrière's unsuspecting readers was this erotico-satiric novel with the come-on title that plays both sides of racial and sexual stereotypes against the middle, and takes fatal and uproarious aim at all manner of sacred cows – including young gifted black writers. Here was a novel by a black man that begins by pronouncing a funeral elegy for the myth of the Great Black Lover. And when Laferrière describes himself and his brothers, he uses the word *nègre* – 'Negro,' or even 'nigger' – instead of the more politically and socially correct *noir* – 'black.' What kind of *Nègre* was this anyway? Not one whom readers, white or black, had met before.

When the novel hit bookstore shelves in Montreal in the fall of 1985, it caused a sensation. Laferrière's ambiguity, and the difficulty of pinning him down, was one of the reasons his book was so infuriating – and so seductive.

Laferrière, meanwhile, was simply following the great tradition of satire, giving students of authorial intention a giant headache. Example: readers on the Left of the political spectrum were condemning this novel for not taking a clear enough stand against racism, even as they recommended it to friends. One critic went after Laferrière for making all his white women English-speaking, not realizing the stereotypical value such things might have for a recent immigrant from Haiti: White = English = America. As Laferrière says in one chapter, 'America is a totality.'

Laferrière knows about the totality of America from the underside. Born in Port-au-Prince, he practiced journalism under Duvalier. When a colleague with whom he was working on a story was found murdered by the roadside, Laferrière took the hint and went into exile in Canada. The year was 1978. He did what most immigrants do: start at the bottom. He worked tanning cowhides in a Montreal factory. *How to Make Love to a Negro* was begun around this time, and when the author says at the end of the novel, 'This book is my last chance,' we can see where he's coming from. That manic energy, that bold and sometimes outrageous tone is that of a man eager to get out of the factory and get some respect, a man suffocating in his social position the way the main character suffocates in his overheated room at 3670, St-Denis. Some immigrants get to the top through commerce of varying sorts. Laferrière, a voracious reader, understands the lesson of the great Jewish-American writers: you can get to the top with words too.

On one level, *How to Make Love to a Negro* is a book about one man's progress as an immigrant. It is, as Leferrière has remarked, the story of a young man who has acquired a culture he was never meant to have; he covets that culture, he wants you to know he's acquired it (hence, punning literary allusions such as the title of Chapter One), but he doesn't want to lose his identity in the meantime. That's where Laferrière parts company with many immigrant novels: the narrator has a distinctly critical eye on the new culture around him, even as he is trying to move into it. Which is another source of ambiguity in the book.

Just as knowing how to manipulate words gets you social mobility, so does making love. *Voilà:* the eternal marriage of sex and artistic creation. The coupling of white women and black man creates a lot of sparks in this book: the attraction of opposites, the potency of guilt, the weight of history. In one episode, the hero of the piece contemplates the Empire-style family portraits on the wall of an ivy-clad dwelling. What am I doing in such a mansion? he wonders, then answers his own question: I am here to take the daughter of the house to bed. Though nothing in his upbringing prepared him for such a cross-class encounter, he is astute enough to note, 'History might not have been good to us. But we can always use it as an aphrodisiac.'

Despite the effective teaser title, in this book sex is mostly an indicator of class, ethnic, and historical conflict. When the hero fails to score, it is because he has committed, not a romantic, but a historical gaffe. Whether it is his praise of carbohydrates to a Scarsdale Diet girl, or his admission that, in his country, people eat cats, the results are hilarious and usually result in the hero sprinting out of his prospective lover's apartment to try to catch the last subway of the night. Even in the most sensual moments, the hero's calm, collected consciousness is evaluating the acts of love-making in terms of class and colour. I suspect that this attitude, more than any erotic description, led that critic in a Trois-Rivières paper to pontificate that Laferrière 'was totally without respect for sexual morality.'

There is another reason for Laferrière's success that has to do with the Quebec writing scene. His book makes an absolute contrast to virtually everything that has been written in Quebec over the last little while. To read this *Nègre*, after suffering through the novels of Jansenist isolation and pent-up madness, the stock in trade of so many Quebec novelists, is more than a breath of fresh air – it's a gale-force wind. Recent Quebec fiction has been so completely fastened to its navel, so lost in grim retrospection, that we can only hope it will never be the same after Laferrière's madcap characters and their excessive energy.

And without burdening this new writer with the 'ethnic' tag, part of the positive response to Laferrière came from the new image he was projecting of an immigrant Quebec. Quebec fiction has always worked with the problems of identity; readers seemed ready to accept Laferrière's immigrant version of that age-old struggle.

A word about the translation of this novel. When I first met Dany Laferrière and discussed the possibility of making an English version of the book, he said, 'It'll be easy. It's already written in English. Just the words are in French.' If only that had been true! The problems started as early as the title. When Laferrière uses the potentially derogatory word, *nègre*, the translator has several choices, but he cannot automatically substitute 'black,' despite what current English usage demands. Our word 'black' is simply too free of stereotypes and too politically cool to be used in social satire. In this book, there are very few occasions when 'black,' the politically correct word, can be used if the translator wants to retain Laferrière's dynamic between the sexes and colours, in which blacks will always be *nègre*. I finally decided on 'Negro,' alternating when the occasion called for it. 'Negro' is outdated, it smells of pre-Black Power liberalism, and because of those echoes it is particularly well suited to Laferrière's satirical intent.

Laferrière is wily, well-read and scheming in the best sense of the word. I believe this new writer deserves our attention and recognition.

– *David Homel*

HOW TO MAKE
LOVE TO A NEGRO

The Nigger Narcissus

I can't believe it, this is the fifth time Bouba's played that Charlie Parker record. He's crazy about jazz, and this must be his Parker period. Last week I had Coltrane for breakfast, lunch and dinner. Now it's Parker's turn.

There's only one good thing about this place: you can play Parker or Miles Davis or even a noisier cat like Archie Shepp at three o'clock in the morning (with walls as thin as onionskin paper) without some idiot telling you to turn it down.

We're suffocating in the summer heat, jammed in between the Fontaine de Johannie (a roach-ridden restaurant frequented by small-time hoods) and a minuscule topless bar, at 3670 rue St-Denis, right across from Cherrier. An abject one-and-a-half that the landlord palmed off on poor Bouba as a two-and-a-half for $120 a month. We're up on the third floor. A narrow room cut lengthwise by a horrible Japanese screen decorated with enormous stylized birds. A fridge in a constant state of palpitation, as if we were holed up above some railroad station. Playboy bunnies thumbtacked to the wall that we had to take down when we got here to avoid the suicidal tendencies those things inevitably cause. A stove with elements as cold as a witch's tit at forty below. And, extra added attraction, the Cross of Mount Royal framed in the window.

I sleep on a filthy bed and Bouba made himself a nest on the plucked couch full of mountains and valleys. Bouba inhabits it fully. He drinks, reads, eats, meditates and fucks on it. He has married the hills and dales of this cotton-stuffed whore.

When we came into possession of this meager pigsty, Bouba settled on the couch with the collected works of Freud, an old dictionary with the letters A through D and part of E missing, and a torn and tattered copy of the Koran.

Superficially, Bouba spends all day doing nothing. In reality, he is purifying the universe. Sleep cures us of all physical impurities, mental illness and moral perversion. Between pages of the Koran, Bouba engages in sleep cures that can last up to three days. The Koran, in its infinite wisdom, states: 'Every soul shall taste death. You shall receive your rewards only on the Day of Resurrection. Whoever is spared the fire of Hell and is admitted to Paradise shall surely gain his end; for the life of this world is nothing but a fleeting vanity.' (Sura III, 182.) The world can blow itself up if it wants to; Bouba is sleeping.

Sometimes his sleep is as strident as Miles Davis' trumpet. Bouba becomes closed upon himself, his face impenetrable, his knees folded under his chin. Other times I find him on his back, his arms forming a cross, his mouth opening onto a black hole, his toes pointed towards the ceiling. The Koran in all its magnanimity says: 'You cause the night to pass into the day, and the day into the night; You bring forth the living from the dead and the dead from the living. You give without stint to whom You will.' (Sura III, 26.) And so Bouba is aiming for a place at the right hand of Allah (may his holy name be praised).

Charlie Parker tears through the night. A heavy, humid, Tristes Tropiques kind of night. Jazz always makes me think of New Orleans, and that makes a Negro nostalgic.

Bouba is crashed out on the couch in his usual position (lying on his left side, facing Mecca), sipping Shanghai tea and perusing a volume of Freud. Since Bouba is totally jazz-crazy, and since he recognizes only one guru (Allah is great and Freud is his prophet), it did not take him long to concoct a complex and sophisticated theory the long and short of which is that Sigmund Freud invented jazz.

'In what volume, Bouba?'

'*Totem and Taboo*, man.'

Man. He actually calls me man.

'If Freud played jazz, for Christ's sake, we would have known about it.'

Bouba breathes in a mighty lungful of air. Which is what he does every time he deals with a non-believer, a Cartesian, a rationalist, a head-shrinker. The Koran says: 'Wait, then, as they themselves are waiting.'

'You know,' Bouba finally intones, 'you know that SF lived in New York.'

'Of course he did.'

'He could have learned to play trumpet from any tubercular musician in Harlem.'

'It's possible.'

'Do you know what jazz is at least?'

'I can't describe it, but I'd know what it is if I heard it.'

'Good,' Bouba says after a lengthy period of meditation, 'listen to this then.'

Then I'm sucked in and swallowed, absorbed, osmosed, drunk, digested and chewed up by a flow of wild words, fantastic hallucinations with paranoid pronunciation, jolted by jazz impulses to the rhythm of Sura incantations – then I realize that Bouba is performing a syncopated, staccato reading of the unsuspecting pages 68 and 69 of *Totem and Taboo*.

The effigy of the Egyptian princess Taiah watches over the ancient couch where Bouba spends his days, horizontal or cross-legged, burning sweet-smelling resins in an Oriental incense-burner. He brews endless cups of tea on an alcohol lamp and reads rare books on Assyrian art, the English mystics, voodoo Vèvès and Swinburne's 'Fata Morgana.' He spends his precious light admiring an engraving, purchased on St. Denis Street, of the fresh body of Dante Gabriel Rossetti's 'Beata Beatrice.'

'Listen to this, man.'

It's the thirtieth time this week I've listened to it. It's a Parker cut. Bouba's face is as tight as a mizzenmast; he's listening to it too. You could hear a tsetse fly buzz. Saint Parker of the Depths, pray for us. I listen as hard as I can. While Bouba literally drinks in every harsh note from Parker's sax. Right in the middle of the Big Phrase (so says Bouba), right when R.I.P. Parker (1920-1955) is about to embark on those precious seconds (128 measures) that revolutionized jazz, love, death and all our goddamn sensibility – the heavens choose to unfurl above our heads in the brutal form of an all-out fuckfest punctuated with strident keening, the cries of wounded beasts, a gut-ripping cavalcade of wild bucking horses, right there, right above our heads. The turn-table jumps like a treetoad with sticky fingers. What's going on? Is this the wrath of Allah? 'Will they not ponder on the Koran? If it had not come from Allah, they could have surely found in it many contradictions.' (Sura IV, 84.) Is it Ogoum, the fire god of the voodoo pantheon? Bouba maintains we have rented the antechamber of hell and that Beelzebub himself lives upstairs. The racket resumes, more violently. Louder. More precipitously. The frenzied gallop of the four horses of the Apocalypse. Parker has just enough time to play 'Cool Blues' and afterwards, that little gem of inventiveness, of audio madness, 'Koko' (1946). The only piece of music that can stand up to this insanity come from on high. The ceiling drops a millimeter in a cloud of pink dust. Then, silence. We wait for the end of the world, impatiently, holding our breath. A private, custom-made Apocalypse. Silence. Then this taut keening cry in high C, sharp and lasting, inhuman, first allegro, then andante, then pianissimo, an endless, inconsolable, electronic, asexual cry over Parker's sax; the only song this dawn.

The Great Mandala
of the Western World

Things are going terribly wrong these days for the conscientious, professional black pick-up artist. The black period is over, has-been, kaput, finito, whited out. Nigger go home. *Va-t-en, Nègre.* The Black Bottom's off the Top 20. *Hasta la vista, Negro.* Last call, coloured man. Go back to the bush, man. Do yourself a hara-kiri you-know-where. Look, Mamma, says the Young White Girl, look at the Cut Negro. A good Negro, her father answers, is a Negro with no balls. In a nutshell, that's the situation in the 1980s, a dark day for Negro Civilization. On the stock market of the Western World, ebony has taken another

spectacular fall. If only the Negro ejaculated oil. Black gold. O
sadness, the Negro's sperm is ivory. Meanwhile, Yellow is
coming on strong. The Japanese are clean, they don't take up
much space and they know the *Kama Sutra* like the back of their
Nikons. The sight of one of those yellow dolls (4 feet 10, 110
pounds), as portable as a make-up case, on the arm of a long,
tall girl (a model or salesgirl in a department store) is enough to
make you cry the blues. I hear the Japs are as good at disco as
Negroes are at jazz. It wasn't always that way. God didn't used
to be yellow – the traitor! During the seventies, America got off
on Red. White girls practically moved onto Indian reservations
to earn their sexual BAs. The co-eds who stayed behind had to
settle for the handful of Indian students still left on the
campuses. Naturally, a great number of Redskins came running
from a great number of tribes, attracted by the scent of young,
white squaw. A young Iroquois had his pride, but a free fuck is
better than a bottle of rotgut. White girls were doing it Huron-
style. A Cheyenne screw was the hottest thing around. Don't
underestimate the effect of fucking a guy whose real name is
Roaring Bull. At night in the dormitories, each cry, according to
its modulation, told of a Huron or an Iroquois or a Cheyenne
inseminating a young white girl with his red jissom. It lasted
until each and every Indian had come down with chronic
syphilis. With the survival of the white Anglo-Saxon race in
danger, the Establishment halted the massacre. WASP girls
received drastic doses of penicillin, and the Indian students
were sent back to their respective reservations to finish the
genocide begun with the discovery of the Americas. The
universities reverted to their daily routine, grey, washed out,
going nowhere, and just as girls were about to succumb to
boredom with the pallid, pale, faded Ivy League boys, the
violent, potent, incendiary Black Panthers burst upon the
campus scene. 'Finally, some real blood!' came a choir of
exultations from the Joyces, Phyllises, Marys and Kays driven
desperate by the medicine-dropper sex of conventional unions
and a grey life of frustration with the Johns, Harrys, Walters and
Company. Fucking black was fucking exotic. And America loves
to fuck exotic. Put black vengeance and white guilt together in
the same bed and you had a night to remember! Those blond-
haired, pink-cheeked girls practically had to be dragged out of

the black dormitories. The Big Nigger from Harlem fucked the stuffing out of the girlfriend of the Razor Blade King, the whitest, most arrogant racist on campus. The Big Nigger from Harlem's head spun at the prospect of sodomizing the daughter of the slumlord of 125th Street, fucking her for all the repairs her bastard father never made, fornicating for the horrible winter last year when his younger brother died of TB. The Young White Girl gets off too. It's the first time anyone's manifested such high-quality hatred towards her. In the sexual act, hatred is more effective than love. But it's all over now. The second war fought on American soil. Compared to the war of the coloured sexes, Korea was a skirmish. And Viet Nam a mere afterthought in the flow of Judeo-Christian civilization. If you want to know what nuclear war is all about, put a black man and a white woman in the same bed. But it's all over now. We came close to total annihilation without knowing it. The black was the last sexual bomb that could have blown up this planet. And now he's dead. Sputtered out between the thighs of a white girl. When you come down to it, the black was just a wet firecracker, but that's not for me to say. Make way for the Yellows. The Japanese are going to take us dancing on the volcano. It's their turn. The great roulette wheel of the flesh. That's how it turns. Red, Black, Yellow. Black, Yellow, Red. Yellow, Red, Black. The Great Mandala of the Western World.

Beelzebub, Lord of the Flies,
Lives Upstairs

Hemingway should be read standing up, Basho walking, Proust in the bath, Cervantes in a hospital, Simenon in a train (Canadian Pacific, anyone?), Dante in paradise, Dosto in the underground, Miller in a smoky bar with hot dogs, fries and a Coke.... I was reading Mishima with a cheap bottle of wine by the bed, totally exhausted, and a girl in the shower.

She stuck her dripping head through the half-open bathroom door and issued two or three rapid requests: a towel to cover her breasts, another to go around her hips (I love Gauguin!), a third for her wet hair and a fourth so she wouldn't have to set foot on the filthy floor.

She came out of the bathroom with a smile. It cost me four towels to see her teeth. I resumed my position, opening Mishima to page 78, and disappeared into pre-war Japan for eighty-eight seconds, good for three and two-thirds pages, before falling into a Fuji bonze Negro sleep.

Sleep is practically impossible in this muggy heat. I left the window open and the hot air completely knocked me out. I'm as groggy as one of those small-time boxers who turn up in Hemingway stories. I don't even have the strength to drag myself to the shower. An ocean of cotton closes around me.

I don't know how long I spent in that state. A distant buzzing awoke me. Airborne above the sink, an enormous green fly with bloodshot eyes is crashing into things. The fly looks blind. Totally drunk on the heat. Frenzied beating of wings. A fly high on codeine. A final collision with the wall and it does a kamikaze dive into the dishwater.

From the horizontal position I consider the cardboard boxes and green garbagebags stuffed with dirty laundry, books, used records and spice bottles that have been cluttering the floor for two days now.

The old fly is inert. It floats on its back. Its pollen-yellow belly swells with water. I pick up Mishima, page 81. The words run like fly streaks. The letters tremble and shimmer. Sentences jump like living things and move before my eyes.

The fly is a stiff corpse drifting among the glasses. I alone am responsible in the eyes of the Lord of the Flies. Bouba maintains that Beelzebub lives upstairs.

The bottle slumps sadly at the foot of the bed. I take a good pull and drift off into sweet somnolence. The wine trickles down my throat, smooth and warm. Not bad for the cheap stuff. I feel soft and sated.

The Negro Is of the
Vegetable Kingdom

1 2 3 4 5 6 7 8 9 10 I get up, steer clear of the shower and give myself a brisk face-wash in the sink. The cold water finishes the slow process of my awakening. Bouba must be on the Mountain checking out the girls getting a tan. The couch resembles an abandoned wife. Bouba will be back later; today is his weekly day out. Bouba is a true hermit. He can spend whole days without even turning on the light. The day passes; Bouba meditates and prays. He wishes to become the purest among pure men. He intends to accept the challenge issued to

Muhammed: 'You cannot make the deaf hear, nor can you guide the blind or those who are in gross error.' (Sura XLIII, 39.)

Miz Literature left me a note, folded in four and stuck in the corner of the mirror. She had almost slipped my mind. She's the McGill girl, the one Bouba nicknamed Miz Literature. That's Bouba's method. The girl we met the other day at a sidewalk café on St. Denis eating ice cream – he called her Miz Sundae. So as not to get Gloria Steinem on our case we say 'Miz.'

Miz Literature used two long paragraphs to tell me she had gone to a 'delicious Greek bakery on Park Avenue.' She's some kind of girl. I met her at McGill, at a typically McGill literary soirée. I let on that Virginia Woolf was as good as Yeats or some kind of nonsense like that. Maybe she thought that was baroque coming from a Negro.

The room is awash in dark sweat. The fly has long since joined his comrades in the great beyond. Above, Beelzebub has been appeased. Green garbagebags litter the middle of the room, their mouths agape. In a box (Steinberg cardboard special), with no semblance of order: a pair of shoes, a box of Sifto iodized salt, turned-up winter boots, a toothbrush, a tube of toothpaste, books, rolled-up Van Gogh reproductions, pens, a pair of sunglasses, a new ribbon for my old Remington and an alarm clock. Idly, I stow it away in a corner, by the fridge. The sun comes slanting through the window in blades of light.

I pile the old newspapers into two stacks. It takes a while to bundle them up, then I stack them at the end of the table. I move silently through the darkness. I've sweated enough for a shower. The bathroom is tiny but at least there's a tub, a sink and a shower – a miracle for this part of town. The old buildings in the *barrio*, if they're lucky enough to have a bathtub, never have a shower.

Miz Literature left her scent in the bathroom. In his journal (*Retour de Tchad*), Gide writes that what struck him most in Africa was the smell. A smell of strong spices. A smell of leaves. The Negro is of the vegetable kingdom. Whites forget that they have a smell too. Most McGill girls smell like Johnson's Baby Powder. I don't know what making love to a girl (over twenty-one, duly vaccinated) who stinks of baby powder does for you. I can never resist going kitchie-kitchie-koo under her chin.

Miz Literature brought her bag of toiletries. *Danger.* What is she after? Is she intent on subletting the single room Bouba and I share? She must have a spacious Outremont apartment, full of light and fresh air and sweet smells, and now she wants to come down here to live! In the heart of the Third World. These infidels are so perverse!

Miz Literature's open bag reveals a toothbrush (there's already a constellation of toothbrushes above my sink), and a tube of Ultra Brite toothpaste (does she think the Negro's sparkling white teeth are pure myth? Well, think again, WASP. No kidding, it's the real thing. Ivory jewels on an ebony ring!). Special soap for dry skin, two tubes of lipstick, an eyebrow pencil, some tampons and a little bottle of Tylenol.

I never go anywhere without my little photo of Carole Laure. Hungry mouth and wide eyes next to the long, soft, refined adolescent face of Lewis Furey. The rich boy, intelligent, sophisticated, gentle, clever as they come – shit! Everything I'd like to be. Starring Carole Laure. Carole Laure starring in my bed. Carole Laure fixing me a tribal dish (spicy chicken and rice). Carole Laure listening to jazz with me in this lousy filthy room. Carole Laure, slave to a Negro. Why not?

Through a microscope, this room would look like a camembert cheese. A forest of odours. The teeming (like the tearing noise of silk paper) of shiny creatures. In summer everything spoils so quickly. A fuckfest of a million germs. I picture the planet that way and among those millions of yellow seeds, I dream of the five hundred out of the five hundred million Chinawomen who would take me for their black Mao.

Cannibalism with a Human Face

A discreet knock-knock-knock at the door. I open. Miz Literature comes in, arms loaded with pâté, croissants, cheese (brie, oka, camembert), smoked sausages, French bread, Greek desserts and a bottle of wine. I make a summary stab at housekeeping, all aglow at the prospect of eating something besides Zorbaburgers or spaghetti à la DaGiovanni.

I throw open the window: dry, burning air pours into the room in waves. I clear the sink of dirty plates and glasses and drain the soapy water. The fly is sucked downward into a better world. 'I swear, by the moon!' (Sura LXXIV, 35.) Farewell, Fly.

Miz Literature finishes cleaning the table. She puts water on to boil for tea. I get comfortable. She fills my glass with wine. I close my eyes. To be waited on by an English girl (Allah is great). Fulfillment is mine. The world is opening to my desires.

I begin to look at Miz Literature with new eyes, though she hasn't changed. She's a tall girl, a little hunched over, with albatross arms, her eyes are a little too bright (too trusting), she has pianist's fingers and a face with astonishingly regular features. Apparently she never had to wear braces, incredible for an Outremont girl. She has small breasts and wears a size 10 shoe.

'Aren't you eating?' I ask her.

'No.'

She answers with a smile. The smile is a British invention. Actually, the British brought it back from one of their Japanese campaigns.

'Don't you want to eat?'

'I'll just watch you,' she breathes.

Just like that, with her eyes on mine.

'I see. You'll just watch me.'

'I'll watch you.'

'You like watching me eat?'

'You have such a good appetite....'

'You're making fun of me.'

'Watching you eat fascinates me. You eat with such passion. I've never seen anyone do it like you do.'

'Is it funny to watch?'

'I don't know. I don't think so. I find it moving, that's all.'

Watching me eat moves her. Miz Literature is incredible. She was brought up to believe everything she's told. Her cultural heritage. I can tell her the most outlandish stories and she'll nod her head and stare with those believing eyes. She'll be moved. I can tell her I consume human flesh, that somewhere in my genetic code the desire to eat white flesh is inscribed, that my nights are haunted by her breasts, her hips, her thighs, I swear it, I can tell her all that and more and she'll understand. She'll believe me. Imagine: she's studying at McGill (venerable institution to which the bourgeoisie sends its children to learn clarity, analysis and scientific doubt) and the first Negro to tell her some kind of fancy tale takes her to bed. Why? Because she can afford that luxury. I surrender to the least bit of naïveté, even for a second, and I'm one dead nigger. Literally. I have to be a moving target, otherwise, at the first emotion, my ass would be grass. Miz Literature can afford a clean clear conscience. She has the means. I gave up on that luxury a long time ago. No conscience. No paradise lost. No promised land. You tell me: what good can a conscience possibly do me? It can only cause problems for a Negro brimming over with unappeased fantasies, desires and dreams. Put it this way: *I want America.* Not one iota less. With her Radio City girls, her buildings, her automobiles, her enormous waste – even her bureaucracy. I want it all: good and bad, what you throw away and what you keep, the ugly and beautiful alike. America is a totality. What do you expect me to do with a conscience? I can't afford one anyway. The way things are going, it would be down at the pawnshop in a flash.

I have to make sure not to bug Miz Literature about being so nice. She's still the best thing a Negro can afford in these hard times of ours.

When the End of the World Comes, We Will Still Be Locked in a Metaphysical Discussion about the Origin of Desire

Bouba emerges from a 72-hour sleep cure and inquires after the health of our planet.
  'What about the bomb?'
  'Not yet.'
  'What are they waiting for?'
  'Your sign, Bouba.'
  'What sign, man?'
  'The Big Sleep.'
  'What keeps you holding on?'

'The thought that there's still plenty of beautiful girls out there, and the illusion that one day I'll have them all.'

'Beauty, beauty.... What's beauty anyway?'

'It's what straightens out a crooked nigger.'

'You've got it all wrong, man. Desire is what gives you that hard-on.'

'Whatever you say, Bouba. But where does desire start in the first place?'

'When you get a hard-on, it's your vision of the world, it's the fantasies of your adolescence and the weather outside that's giving you a hard-on. Beauty has nothing to do with it.'

'But a nice ass....'

'Only in your mind, man.'

'Ass exists only in my mind?'

'Sure, man. Here's the proof: when you make love with a girl and she's on her back, you don't even see that mythological ass.'

'We don't all do it the same way.'

'Don't confuse the issue – we always go back to that missionary thing. All right, let's take the mouth. You meet a girl in the street. She has a sensual, hungry mouth, the whole package. You tell her this and that, she answers that and this, and a couple hours later you're kissing. But when you're kissing you can't see her mouth. When you're up that close you can't see anything at all.'

'All right, you kiss her with your imagination, I go along with you there. But when you kiss her you've got this picture of her mouth in your mind, that's why you wanted to kiss her in the first place. At the moment of the kiss, desire is consummated.'

'But the mouth in your mind, your ideal mouth, is better than the real mouth, the mouth that belongs to the girl you happened to meet on such-and-such a street at such-and-such a time. At the last minute she could change mouths and you wouldn't be any wiser.'

'That's ridiculous, Bouba. Who's ever changed mouths?'

'For the sake of argument, man.'

'You're one Cartesian nigger!'

'*You're* the Cartesian, man. *I'm* a Freudian: a goddamned Freudian nigger.'

'What have you got against Beauty anyway?'

Bouba is sitting on the couch now. The debate shakes his entire being. He debates with his body. Seeing him sweat, you smell him. Suddenly his words start pouring out. He's like a tiger with a whiff of blood in his nostrils. The blood of his next victim. My blood. Nose to the ground, he sniffs his idea back to its source. He pretends he didn't hear my question. I know him too well. There's nothing wrong with his hearing. His mind is just as acute. He doesn't think like other people. He thinks against them. He has a personal vision of things and he expresses it with his long, supple, fragile hands. As he speaks they sketch arabesques as strange and astonishingly complex as ideograms. At first it looks as though he's shooing flies with those endless hands like dowagers' fans, but when you look closer and listen to his words, you see the organic link between the idea and the dance of his hands. Slender, sophisticated hands that have never worked. The hands of an old mandarin. Which makes for a rather baroque atmosphere. Two blacks in a filthy apartment on the rue St-Denis, philosophizing their heads off about Beauty in the wee hours. The Repast of the Primitives. The kettle is boiling. We have no radio, no TV, no telephone, no newspapers. Nothing to keep us in touch with this lousy planet. History is not interested in us and we repay the favour. It's even steven. All that matters is this grave and gratuitous conversation between me and that crazy ape-man Bouba. The fate of Judeo-Christian civilization is on the line. Two blacks on the dole hold the keys. We are discussing matters of life and death and Bouba, hirsute of head, confers a certain mystique to our confabulation. Bouba is lost in thoughts dangerous to his mental health. He wants to talk me into a verbal pulp. He can argue all night over the sex of angels. (Talking about angels, especially the fallen kind, I haven't heard from Beelzebub for some time now. I wonder what he's up to up there.) Nothing can resist Bouba's manic lucidity. His face becomes distorted with tics, his eyes two round, brilliant marbles. Horizontal on the ancient couch. Just before daybreak, you come to appreciate his terrifying rhetorical machine. Endless argumentation broken by fits of coughing. His monologue can last for hours, flowing uninterrupted, serpentine, snaking, sinuous, Proustian sentences like a long, many-coloured ribbon. The Word is his poison. With his narrow, bare chest, his hair in revolt and his beard narrowing to a point, he looks like an Old Testament prophet. ('By the declining star, I swear!' Sura LIII, 1.) I picture him as the last man on this barren planet after the nuclear blast, his words flowing endlessly, considering the decor as no more than a minor annoyance.

'What do I have against Beauty?'

Bouba savours the question. It's right up his alley. The kind of question that sets off a Boston marathon of words. A question that pushes and tugs, the kind of thing you can change the world with. 'What do I have against Beauty?' Bouba scratches his chin. His nervous tic. It signifies, Here is a question you do not answer lightly. Bouba pours himself more tea. He's in no hurry. He has plenty of time. Eternity is on his side. Outside, people are stirring, awakening, getting their clothes on, gulping down breakfast and rushing off to work. Brainless ants. The world is in terrible need of marginal thinkers, starving philosophers and impenitent sleepers ('The sleeping man reconstructs the world,' said Heraclitus) to keep on spinning. Bouba spends most of his time on the couch reconstructing the world. Today, he will attack one of the Western World's last bastions: Beauty.

'Here's the problem, man: Beauty is shameless.'

'Great! I've got a nigger moralist on my hands now.'

'It's thermodynamic, man, not moral. There's a certain temperature that determines the degree of desire we feel for someone. The heat can go in two directions, inside and out.'

'All right. Then what?' I still don't trust Bouba's demonstration.

'Beauty's heat goes only to the outside.'

'What's wrong with that?'

'I prefer implosion to explosion.'

'I don't think I get it.'

'All subtlety is lost on a guy like you.' In a discussion, Bouba acts as if I'm a complete stranger. 'All right, take Miz Beauty. She thinks she's doing you a favour by fucking with you, while with Miz Piggy, you're doing her the favour, and that makes all the difference in the world.'

'Altruist!'

'Not at all. The relation is different – and to my advantage.'

'Is that so?'

'Haven't you ever made love to a big ugly girl who's half moron and up to her fat neck in complexes? Pure ecstasy, man. Non-stop whispering in your ear, what a great man you are, all that. But try making love to one of these Brooke Shields clones: all she wants is compliments, talk to me, talk to me, the famous 'talk to me' people talk about so much, which boils down to *I Demand Compliments.* Only Allah is worthy of such praise. The Koran says, 'Praise Allah morning and night.' Miz Beauty does not speak. You've got to discover her erogenous zones, her favourite subjects of conversation, her sign, all on your own. Meanwhile, Miz Piggy's coming like an express train. She doesn't get it every day. And she's hell-bent to make the most of it. She wants more, more, more. And *that*, man, is the true foundation of fucking. The rest is representation, pure fashion show, masturbation on a glossy page from *Vogue.*'

'What if you end up with an ugly girl who's no good?'

'That could only happen to you, man.'

If I understand correctly, the couch is one of those fat girls seething with complexes who's great in bed. When you consider the couch with a minimum of sensitivity, you realize what Bouba's practiced eye saw all along. The couch is endowed with the open, luxuriant forms of Rubens' women. Standing before his canvases, who has not dreamed of such fleshly immersion? Such generous smooth bodies?

Bouba drains his teacup and goes quietly back to bed like a black maharajah in his St. Denis harem. Let the world hurl itself towards nuclear culmination. Bouba is sleeping.

Must I Tell Her That a Slum
Is Not a Salon?

Miz Literature comes sweeping in with an enormous bouquet of peonies. I'm still in bed with Bukowski. The window is closed. A line of sunlight cuts the page in half lengthwise.

I read lying down with a pillow between my shoulderblades and my head slightly raised. Stiff neck guaranteed. Unfortunately, it's my favourite position. Usually I read early in the morning before it gets too hot, when I'm not likely to be disturbed. The building emanates an aura of calm. My neighbours, retired for the most part, are not yet awake. In an hour or two it'll be the breakfast routine, the whistling of the pipes, the tap of toothbrushes and the smell of bacon.

I watch Miz Literature move through the shadows. It looks like she's wearing a yellow dress with a white collar. And ballerina shoes. I picture her dressing with care, putting on perfume (just a soupçon!) and her bra (she has small breasts) so she can go do dishes for a Negro in a filthy apartment on St. Denis near the Carré St. Louis. Skid row. Miz Literature comes from a good family, she has a bright future, upright values, a solid education, perfect mastery of Elizabethan poetry, she belongs to a feminist literary club at McGill – the McGill Witches – whose mission is to restore the reputation of unjustly neglected poetesses. This year they are publishing a luxury edition of Emily Dickinson with ink drawings by Valery Miller. So what's going on here? You could hold a gun to her head and she wouldn't do the tenth of what she does here for a white guy. Miz Literature is writing her PhD thesis on Christine de Pisan. Which is no mean feat. So what the hell is she doing in this filthy slum? And don't blame Cupid. If she were madly in love with a McGill guy he'd never ask her to do the tenth of what she does here, spontaneously, freely and graciously.

'Why do the dishes now?'

'Am I disturbing you?'

'Not really.'

'You're reading! Oh, I'm sorry.'

And believe it or not, she really is sorry. Reading is sacred in her book. Besides, a black with a book denotes the triumph of Judeo-Christian civilization! Proof that those bloody crusades really did have some value. True, Europe did pillage Africa but this black is reading a book.

'There, I finished.'

She puts the clean dishes away carefully. A real jewel. Her only shortcoming is that she'll go to any length to make this room pleasant. Confer an Outremont touch to it. Every time she comes she brings something new. Pretty soon, in a few months, we'll be crushed under the weight of rare vases, engravings, bedside lamps and all that crap you can buy in those snobby boutiques on Laurier Street. McGill people are taught to decorate their environment. Look what I've gotten myself into! All right, I can understand that part. But I don't get why she's doing it here in this slum. Must I tell her that a slum is not a salon? Maybe it's part of her double life. By day a WASP princess; by night slave to a Negro. That could be exciting. Suspense guaranteed because with Negroes you never know. Let's just eat her up right now, yum-yum, with a little salt and pepper. I can see the headlines in *La Presse*.

THE TALK OF THE TOWN –
    'DID YOU HEAR? TWO BLACKS ATE A MCGILL CO-ED.'
    'HOW DID THEY DISCOVER THE CRIME?'
    'THE POLICE FOUND HER ARM IN THE REFRIGERATOR.'
    'OH, GOOD LORD! IS THAT THE NEW IMMIGRATION POLICY?
IMPORTING CANNIBALS?'
    'I SUPPOSE THEY RAPED HER FIRST, WHILE THEY WERE AT IT?'
    'WE'LL NEVER KNOW. THEY ATE EVERYTHING.'
    'OH, GOOD LORD'

Miz Literature climbs into my bed. I put the book down at the foot of the bed, next to the bottle of wine, then bring her down to my level. Europe has paid her debt to Africa.

And Now Miz Literature Is
Giving Me Some Kind of Blow Job

Miz Literature pours water into a ceramic vase she brought yesterday, then carefully arranges the flowers. She opens the window and places the vase in the left-hand corner, just above my head.

Miz Literature is standing on the bed and her long legs, sheathed in mocha stockings, bring visions of the Golden Gate. The sun is with us now. Hot air fills the room. I drop the book to the floor and pull Miz Literature to me.

Miller says there is nothing better than making love at noon. Miller is right.

If you think you're about to be served up a hot slice of Miz Literature's sexual proclivities, think again. You've got your choice of porno novels for that. I recommend the Midnight series. Miz Literature says I make love the way I eat. With the hunger of a man stranded on a desert island. When you think about it, that's no compliment. Strange, but she says I remind her of an innocent child who has been mistreated too long. She likes making love to me. After the storm has passed, she holds me in her arms. I doze off. On her white breast. I am her child. An untrusting child, so hard sometimes. Her black boy. She strokes my forehead. Happy, gentle, fragile moments. I am more than Black. She is more than White.

If she had been giving me a blow job, I would have had my cock lopped off. Oof! Cut clean off! This time the ceiling fell in – literally, in a cloud of pink dust. Beelzebub is pulling out all the stops upstairs. A fuck to the death. Miz Literature has never attended one of Beelzebub's demonstrations. The galloping ghost. The Horsemen of the Apocalypse. The ceiling opening up. We're rooted to the spot and in our minds, the terrifying image of a couple fucking crushing a couple in repose. The Koran says, 'Tell me, if the scourge of Allah overtook you unawares or openly, would any perish but the transgressors?' (Sura VI, 47.)

Miz Literature has been staring straight ahead since it began. Hypnotized. Her lips tremble slightly. A contraction at one corner of her mouth.

Upstairs Beelzebub is going back for second helpings. Miz Literature is as red as a boiled lobster. I'm sure she's going to drop from a stroke. They're tearing each other apart upstairs. A super-performance. Shamefully, I must face the fact: I start to get hard again. White, right and proper, Miz Literature glances surreptitiously at my penis. The snaking veins begin to uncoil. A serpent's head rising. The Koran says, 'Men, have fear of your Lord, who created you from a single soul. From that soul He created its mate, and through them He bestrewed the earth with countless men and women. Fear Allah, in whose name you plead with one another, and honour the mothers who bore you. Allah is ever watching over you.' (Sura IV, 1.) I cannot countenance this thing that abases me. No doubt, man is an unnatural animal. The Koran asks, 'How many generations have We destroyed before them! Can you find one of them still alive,

or hear so much as a whisper from them?' I try to think
unpleasant thoughts; I think of *The Critique of Pure Reason*.
Kant becomes porno. *The Critique* gives me a hard-on. It grows.
Miz Literature stares straight ahead. We hear the double gasp of
Beelzebub and his accomplice. Like a slow dance. They're doing
it in slow motion. In some movies they show the violent parts in
slow motion to increase the effect. Like violence shot into our
blood. A hypodermic. In our veins. We sense their movements in
a mad modern ballet. Two naked bodies violently intertwined in
a pas de deux of death. My sex keeps rising, obeying a secret
command beyond my will. Miz Literature turns slightly on her
axis, watching it rise with a disconcerting stare. She lowers
herself towards me, reducing the angle to fifteen degrees. In the
sitting position. Her eyes still staring. I close mine and Miz
Literature, in a trance, takes me in her mouth. Between her
beautiful pink lips. I'd dreamed of it. I'd licked my chops over it.
I didn't dare ask her. An act so.... I knew that as long as she
hadn't done it, she wouldn't be completely mine. That's the key
in sexual relations between black and white: as long as the
woman hasn't done something judged degrading, you can never
be sure.

Because in the scale of Western values, white woman is
inferior to white man, but superior to black man. That's why she
can't get off except with a Negro. It's obvious why: she can go as
far as she wants with him. The only true sexual relation is
between unequals. White women must give white men pleasure,
as black men must for white women. Hence, the myth of the
Black stud. Great in bed, yes, but not with his own woman. For
she has to dedicate herself to his pleasure. Upstairs, Beelzebub
is back for another go-round. And now Miz Literature is giving
me some kind of blow job. I think of the faraway village where I
was born. Of all those blacks who travelled to a white man's
land in search of riches and came back empty-handed. I don't
know why – it has nothing to do with what's going on – but I
think of a song I heard years ago. A guy in my village had a
Motown record. The song was about a lynching. The lynching in
St. Louis of a young black man. He was hanged then castrated.
Why castrated? I'll never stop wondering about that. Why
castrated? Can you tell me? Of course no one wants to get
involved with a question like that. I'd love to know, I'd like to be

one hundred percent sure whether the myth of the animalistic, primitive, barbarous black who thinks only of fucking is true or not. Evidence. Show me evidence. Definitively, once and for all. No one can. The world has grown rotten with ideologies. Who will risk taking a position on a subject like that? As a black, I don't have enough distance. Are black men sensual pigs? Are white men pale pigs? Yellow men refined pigs? Red men bleeding pigs? Only Pig is Pig. I don't know why I always imagined the universe like that Matisse painting. Something about it struck me. It's my essential vision of things. I'm talking about 'Grand Intérieur Rouge' (1948). Primary colours. Strong, alive, violent and loud. Pictures inside a larger canvas. Everywhere flowers in different-sized pots. On two tables. A dark chair. On the wall a painting by the artist (the pineapple one) separated by a black demarcation. Under the table, a calico cat chased by a dog. Stylized, allusive strokes. Splashes of bright colour. The skins of two beasts under the curved legs of the table on the right. The painting is primitive, animal, gregarious, fierce, flighty, tribal fantasy. You can feel a playful kind of cannibalism verging on immediate happiness. Right there, before your eyes. With those loud, primary colours and violent sexuality (despite the calm the eye feels) offering a new version of love in this modern jungle. When I ask myself hard questions about the role of colour in sexuality, I remember Matisse's answer. I have been carrying it with me ever since. I didn't yet know it would not be enough to counter the storms of life, and that I would probably die with the teeth of that problem sunk into my neck.

Without warning I send a strong stream of come in Miz Literature's face. She throws her head back and I catch a strange glow in her eyes. She dives down for my penis like a piranha. She sucks. I get hard. She gets on top. This isn't one of those innocent, naive, vegetarian fucks she's used to. We're two carnivores in bed. Miz Literature issues two or three high-pitched moans. Any minute, the vase of peonies above us is going to fall and split our heads open. I'm making love at the edge of the abyss. Miz Literature squats down in a dirty position and moves slowly up and down the length of my cock. A dusky mast. Her head is completely thrown back. Her breasts pointing to the ceiling and her mouth a painful smile. I caress her hips, her sweaty torso and the titillated tips of her breasts. Suddenly her body is racked by hard, rapid shocks and a low growl issues from her throat.

'Fuck me!'

Jesus Christ, that's the limit! Here I am worrying about that animal Beelzebub who reduces sexuality to the animal level, and all the time he was just screaming out loud what Miz Literature always wanted to say.

'You're my man!'

I turn her over on her back. She is laid out as soft and pliable as a ragdoll. Her eyes sightless.

'Wait,' she breathes.

'Is everything all right?'

'You're the first man I've ever said that to.'

'Huh?'

'I want to be yours.'

We made love again. Miz Literature got up an hour later and went to take a shower. She's an hour and a half late for her class. She has to go back home first, change, then hurry to McGill. I stay in bed. No showers for me after love-making. I keep the smells. I open Bukowski's book. Miz Literature kisses me chastely on the forehead then leaves with a final, astonished glance at the couch where Bouba still sleeps, mouth wide open and arms crossed over his chest.

Miz Afternoon on Her
Radiant Bicycle

With great ceremony, I remove the dust cover from the old
Remington 22. The machine gives me a nasty look. We haven't
seen each other for a long time. The machine is sulking. I had it
in pawn for a while. To cheer it up (there's nothing worse than
working on a depressed typewriter), I give it a good cleaning. I
oil it with petroleum jelly. The Remington shines like a wild
rosebush in the rain. My work table (which is also the dining
room table, the spare chair and a makeshift bed when the desire
arises) faces a narrow partition, away from the window. Behind
the wall across the way is the room of a professional cyclist who

spends night and day polishing his heap. Slowly, daylight enters the room. I flip open the Remington's top and replace the ribbon. The cursor moves as smooth as silk. I slip a white sheet of paper in the roller, move my chair in front of the machine, settle in with a bottle of cheap wine at my feet and, once the ritual is over, I put my chin on my palm, dreaming as we all do of being Ernest Hemingway.

Three hours later, the page as white as ever, I decide to clean house (sweeping, cleaning, the dishes) as proof that genius can express itself in a variety of ways. Waves of heat flood in through the window. I pile the books in a corner under the table and stow the typewriter under the bed.

The room is a pigsty. I've said it before and I'll say it again. I sweep up wherever the broom will reach and take down the trash. You could bake in this room. The room smells of sulphur and the whole place could burst into flames at any minute. I pick up bottles from under the table, the bed and the couch. I go down to Pellatt's and get ten cents each from the guy behind the counter. Ah, America, America, America! ('On the day we call a witness from every nation, their pleas shall not avail the unbelievers, nor shall they be allowed to make amends.' Sura XVI, 85.) Nothing like routine to get you back in shape. I decide to do my change of address at the post office on St. Catherine Street. I go down St. Denis to St. Catherine and turn towards Radio-Québec. The air is quivering with heat. Strike a match and all Montreal will go up. I walk slowly. Just ahead of me, a girl comes out of Hachette with Miller under her arm and almost nothing on her back. My temperature shoots up to 120. It's 90 degrees in the shade. The slightest spark and I'll blaze like a slum on a Rio hillside. I warned myself to be careful. Every summer I go crazy like this, and a girl eating ice cream is always to blame. Miz Bookstore's flavour is raspberry. In the final analysis, what's a girl with ice cream except someone who is hungry or thirsty? But in the summertime it's more than that. Just as I was about to fall in love with Miz Bookstore, I see another girl gliding down the street on her radiant bicycle, whistling. I stop breathing. She brakes and stops at the corner. Red light: her left foot on the pavement, her back bent gracefully, the nape of her neck exposed. Girls like to keep their hair short in the summer. Her body like a bent bow. Green light: she shoves off with her right foot on the pedal. Her body like the arrow that flies. Last image: her back a pure line, the graceful movement of her hips, her slender, adolescent thighs. The emotion: the pain of losing someone forever whom you've loved totally, if only for twelve and three-tenths seconds.

There's a long line at the post office. We're packed in like sardines. I check out the sardine in front of me. She's reading a book. This particular sardine is book-crazy. Whenever I see someone reading, I have to know what book, if it's good, what it's about.
    'What's it about?'
    'What's what about?'
    'Your book.'
    'It's a novel.'
    'What kind?'
    'Science fiction.'
    'Is it good?'
    'It's okay.'
    'You don't like it?'
    'I don't know.'
    'What's wrong with it?'
    She brushes aside her red hair. Some women's eyes scare you. She's been over-cruised and she's sick of it.
    'What do you want anyway?'
    She's talking loud.
    'Nothing, nothing.'
    'Leave me alone, all right?'
    'Forget it,' I stammer.
    Most of the people in line have turned around to watch the spectacle of the Negro attacking the white woman. One girl with a shaved head up towards the front of the line wheels around, rage in her breast. She raises her voice to tell everyone how we're all maniacs, psychopaths and hassle-artists who are always coming on to women. 'They're never around in winter but when summer comes they crawl out of their holes, whole bunches of them, to hassle people with their scarves and drums and bracelets and bells. The hell with their folklore! And it's not just the niggers! Now we've got the Latinos with their chains

around their necks, their necklaces, their rings, their broaches, pushing baubles on us in the cafés. If it's not a fake Mayan jewel, it's their body. That's all those Latins thank about.' At first the audience agrees with the shaved-head girl; who among them hasn't been importuned by a folkloric cruise? But to attack the trade of those poor South Americans and the tradition of the Negroes is going too far.

A man in his forties jumps in. Your typical union man. Worn face. 'You can't be prejudiced,' he says, 'lots of guys hassle women and not all of them are black. If you think that about blacks, what do you think they think about us? We colonized them! Sure, coming onto a woman is degrading for her, but it's an innocent game compared to the slave trade.' For a moment everyone is too shocked by the perversity of the argument to react. Once they get over it, the shaved-head girl counterattacks. 'Tell me about it! The colonizers played out their phallic domination fantasies by crushing other people and now that the time's come to pay the bill, this bastard is offering our women for the niggers to fuck.' Our women! She said our women. Everyone must think she's a lesbian defending her territory.

Finally, I manage to change my address. I stroll down St. Catherine. The heat is intolerable. I go into a bank building, cool with air conditioning, and guess who I see: Miz Shaved Head with the girl from the post office. She got her. Cruising is practically impossible with that kind of unfair competition.

A Remington 22
That Belonged to Chester Himes

Bouba came back from the store. Except for some dehydrated potatoes and rotten onions, we had run out of provisions. Bouba fell for the Pellatt's special: a pork shoulder at $1.09 a pound, fresh green onions at $2.39, six boxes of Campbell's Soup at 29 cents each, dish soap (we were in dire need) for $1.87, a carton of creamy margarine (disgusting) for 59 cents and, at the regular price, a kilo of iodized salt, a 25-pound sack of Uncle Ben's rice and three cans of spaghetti.

Bouba is making chicken and rice with peanut sauce. The smell is inspirational. I sit down at the typewriter in hopes of forcing something out of a Remington 22 that actually saw Joan Baez in the flesh. I bought the machine at a junkshop on Ontario Street that sells pedigreed typewriters. Old machines. The guy sells them to young writers. Who else but a young writer would be foolish enough to go for such an obviously commercial ploy? Who else would consider himself a writer just because he owned a machine that belonged to Chester Himes, James Baldwin or Henry Miller? This guy pitches his machines according to the kind of book you want to write. If it's a paranoid book, he'll sell you the schizophrenic machine that belonged to Tennessee Williams. If you're looking for a suicide machine, there's Mishima's old model. For those in the family saga game, Joyce Carol Oates' Olivetti will do the trick. Want to write a bestseller? Step right up and purchase the solid gold heap that Puzo owned. And if you're interested in the tangled destinies of a young Southerner and his neighbours (a Jewish genius and a disturbed young Polish girl), take Bill Styron's Corona. How can one choose among this embarrassment of riches? It's like Ali Baba's cave for a young writer. The junkman's voice left me no repose, praising Salinger's discreet machine, Gabrielle Roy's tin one, the prudish machine of Virginia Woolf, etc. Here's the terrorist machine that the Black Panthers used to type their communiqués – it's a portable, of course. The choice boiled down to Hemingway's old Underwood and the Remington 22 that belonged to Chester Himes. I took Himes.

I've always had this old shoebox full of notebooks, with a journal I've kept on and off for three years, and stacks of cards where I note down sentences that come to me, sketches, bits of dialogue overheard in bars, short descriptions of chance encounters, objects and animals, thoughts on jazz, girls, hunger – that sort of thing. A kind of autobiographical grab-bag where the beginning of a novel, an unfinished journal and a missed appointment are all thrown together. What can be saved from this amorphous mass? Burning it is the only reasonable thing to do. I dry out the sink, set the box in it and prepare for immolation. ('Ta ha. It was not to distress you that we revealed the Koran.' Sura XX, 1.)

The chicken and rice is ready. I set the table. Bouba puts on a Coleman Hawkins record (*Blues for Yolande*) that he cut with Ben Webster.

'You writing, man?'

'I'm trying.'

'What's it about?'

Bouba never reads what I write. He likes to talk about it, build a project, discuss a subject, but reading a manuscript – never. He abhors being presented with a fait accompli.

'I think I'm onto something big.'

'Great!' Bouba looks happy. 'Tell me about it.'

'It's a novel.'

'No kidding.... A novel? A real novel?'

'Well ... a short novel. Not a real novel – more like fantasies.'

'Knock it off, man. Leave that number to the disabused, used-up critics who don't have any more juice. A novel's a novel. Short or long. Tell me about it.'

'There's nothing to it. It's about a guy, a black, who lives with a friend who spends all day lying on a couch meditating, reading the Koran, listening to jazz and screwing when it comes along.'

'Does it come along?'

'I suppose it does.'

'Hey, man, I like that, I really do. I like the idea of the guy who doesn't do fuck-all.'

'Of course you do. You're my model.'

'Writers! You can't trust them, they're all bastards!'

Bouba lets loose a big jazz laugh.

'Then what happens?'

'Nothing in particular.'

Hawkins' sax plays 'Body and Soul' (1939).

Cruising in Place

Miz Literature arrives just in time with a cheesecake in a white box tied with a pink ribbon. Bouba produces some wine dregs he's been hiding in one of the folds of the couch. We wash it down. Miz Literature can't stay too long. She has a class tonight. I like these whirlwind visits.

Miz Literature takes a little wine. Two fingers. She's one of these giddy drunks. She dances across the room with all the grace of an albatross, running into the couch, the table, the fridge, and the Japanese screen. She takes off her shoes and throws them at the ceiling. Then it's on with the dance, with awkward strength and transparent joy. She is wearing a white dress with a black collar and charcoal tights. The floor is littered with butts and stained with drying puddles of beer. Miz Literature dances on, unaware of the filth. She's a flower on a dung-heap. Then she slows down and collapses on the couch next to Bouba, with her arms crossed.

'You know what, Bouba,' she says, 'I mentioned you to my friend Valery and she doesn't believe me.'

'What doesn't she believe?'

'She doesn't believe you exist.'

Miz Literature looks at Bouba with the eyes of a Bodhisattva.

'I told her you were Montreal's only living saint. I told her you live like a monk, that you hardly eat and that you only drink tea.'

'Is that the low-down on me?'

'Your life is clarity. You spend it sleeping on this couch when you're not reading the Koran.'

'Is she ugly at least, this rare pearl of yours?'

'Oh, no! She's beautiful!'

'Then you might as well forget it.'

Miz Literature wasn't expecting that. She stood there open-mouthed a minute. I was busy at my machine, correcting the chapter I had just finished. It was a mild afternoon. The shoebox, belly exposed, was on the table. A fly landed on the cake like a raisin. Miz Literature looked to me for an explanation.

'Didn't you know?'

'Know what?' she asked.

'Didn't you know Bouba is scared stiff of Beauty?'

'Oh, God! When Valery hears that she'll go crazy. She's always dreamed of meeting someone who cared about more than her looks.'

Miz Literature pours herself more wine. She's in a great mood today. I love the gaiety of serious girls. There's a knock on the door. Miz Literature smiles mischievously.

'I asked Valery to pick me up here.'

Three discreet little knocks. McGill code, it would seem. Miz Literature opens the door and a magnificent girl walks in. The kind of girl who leaves you breathless. Her smile is warm. Not that she needed it to set this room on fire. Bouba remains impassive. Miz Literature does the introductions. Bouba looks out the window. The evening shimmers. He takes down his old hunting hat. It's his day to go out.

I swear by the Exordium ('Praise be to Allah, Lord of the Creation') that was the most electrifying cruise I have ever witnessed. Once Bouba's out the door, Valery literally goes into convulsions. She's one of those girls, not a snob or anything, whom everyone cruises but who refuses to go out with anyone. I'm sure McGill is full of very rich, very handsome and very intelligent fools whose only dream is to marry her. To meet Valery is to understand the dilemma: she despises herself, her beauty, wealth and intelligence – the classic situation! Her beauty stands between her and Truth, so she thinks. When you come down to it, Valery is looking for a guru. Bouba the Guru. Wouldn't you know it: to get the most beautiful girl at McGill, you have to stay at home and do nothing. Cruising in place.

Miz Suicide on the Couch

Bouba is sitting on the couch like an ancient bhikkhu
deciphering Li Po ideograms, with Miz Suicide at his feet,
drinking in his words. Behold Miz Suicide: a tall stringy girl with
dishwater hair and eyes that are always open a little too wide.
Bouba is her suicide consultant. Suicide is her only interest. And
the world returns the favour, with the exception of Bouba, who
receives her every Tuesday and Thursday, from 4:00 to 4:45 p.m.,
which makes for three teas at fifteen minutes each.

Miz Suicide brews her own tea in an old samovar, heating up
the water on an alcohol lamp. Miz Suicide, you guessed it,

journeys through life with a pack of Camels, dirty fingernails and a copy of *The Prophet* by Khalil Gibran. Bouba unearthed her at the Esoteric Bookstore on St. Denis, across from the Bibliothèque Nationale.

Seated on the couch like a diva in endless improvisation on the phrases of the old Zen master, Bouba creates a singular atmosphere without even trying. In his guttural, mystic voice, he reads the slender, precious book by the bearded poet Li Po on the correct manner of drinking tea.

'First you must learn,' Bouba explains, 'how to breathe the tea before proceeding to drink it.'

Miz Suicide listens with the inner concentration of a true bodhisattva.

'Like this?'

'No. Let the bouquet of the tea slowly flow into you.'

Conscientiously, Miz Suicide sticks her nose into the teacup. When she comes up for air, her steamy nose is a horrible sight to see, as if she had just escaped drowning.

'Now,' Bouba instructs her, 'you may take the first sip.'

'Not yet,' she says, more fanatic than her master, 'I want to breathe it some more.'

I lie back on the bed, trying to clear the thoughts from my head. Coleman is playing 'Blues Connotation.' Bouba speaks in low tones. Miz Suicide drinks her tea with ecstatic expression. I open the window. Down below in the alley, some kids are playing hockey. Six boys, three girls. From up here they look short and squat. The biggest girl is strong but the little one is not really old enough to play. She is too busy hanging onto her dog so he won't disturb the game. The dog is stronger than she is and he drags her into the fray. She pulls back on the leash, then gives up and drops it. The dog rushes into the melee and grabs the puck from off a stick. Then, according to a well-rehearsed ritual, the dog comes back and drops the puck on the girl's lap. He lays his head in her lap and whimpers. The angry players recover the puck. The girl reprimands the whimpering dog. She pets him. The dog lets himself be petted for a minute or two, then rushes off to disrupt the game again. Darkness settles. The game slows down. The players are tired. The Cross on the Mountain is phosphorescent.

Coleman, side B. I've been sitting in front of this machine for ten minutes, trying to coax something out of a Remington that belonged to Chester Himes. Bouba and Miz Suicide continue their timeless dialogue. I seek inspiration from the struggles of a cockroach in the sink. ('No mortal eyes can see Him, though he sees all eyes. He is benignant and all-knowing.') Coleman's jazz ushers the insect into death. Upstairs, Beelzebub will not forgive us for this latest murder. Miz Suicide gets up for more tea and turns on the water. The Angel of Death.

Bouba sits bare-chested on the couch.

'Do you know Papini?'

'No,' answers Miz Suicide.

'Papini,' Bouba lets on, 'wrote some very intelligent things on the subject of suicide.'

'What did he say?'

Miz Suicide's only suitor is death.

'You see,' Bouba begins, 'this Papini was an Italian writer, a totally disillusioned man. In one of his books, he tells the story of a German who wanted to commit suicide.'

Miz Suicide listens like a bodhisattva of the highest degree.

'This gentle, civilized man sought a courteous way of killing himself,' Bouba continues.

'What did he do?'

'He analyzed the methods. He considered all of them brutal, stupid or vulgar, except one....'

'Yes? ...'

Miz Suicide is feverish with suspense.

'This one: he decided to let himself waste away, physically and morally, day after day.'

'But millions of people do that!'

'Of course. The difference is that he did it methodically.'

An angel passes. A death-angel. Miz Suicide shakes her head. Bouba smiles beatifically. Coleman blows. A pause. Then Miz Suicide drinks her final sip of tea, packs her grip in silence and leaves.

'You really think that empty shell understood your Sermon on the Mount, you bum-wipe Buddha?' I asked him a little later.

'Why not?'

'Aren't you afraid she'll really go and do it one day?'

'On the contrary, man: it's the only thing that keeps her alive.'

'It's the only thing that lets you play black Buddha.'

Bouba breaks out in seismic laughter.

'What are you doing with that bag of bones anyway?'

'Ever heard of charity, man?'

'You don't know the first thing about Buddhism, you Buddha-hole.'

'How dare you say that?'

'You know what the Diamond Sutra says, brother: Charity is but a word.'

Bouba lets loose another dissonant jazz laugh (a kind of scream shot through with honks).

'The hell with the Diamond Sutra. No Sutra can stand up to the Buddha.'

A Bouquet of Lilacs
Sparkling with Rain

Tap, tap, tap, on the door. Very discreet.

'Can we come in?'

'If you're bringing cold hard coin of the realm – otherwise, keep walking.'

'We're bringing flowers.'

There's a girlish burst of laughter and the two of them come in, each carrying a bouquet. Bouba has been sleeping for several hours, legs pressed against his chest, in the fetal position. Valery Miller makes a beeline for the couch with a big bouquet of lilacs sparkling with rain. Miz Literature puts her flowers in a vase and the vase in a corner of the window ledge. She watches me type for a moment. Valery Miller is wearing a green and yellow Sonia Delaunay-style dress.

'What are you writing?'

'A novel.'

'A novel!'

'Fantasies, really.'

'Fantasies!'

In the Western world the word 'fantasy' is the next most powerful thing after the atom bomb.

Outside, a fine slanting rain is falling. Not enough to cool the air.

Valery Miller seems right at home here, standing by the window, gazing at the Cross. Even that lousy Cross looks a little more human when it's being looked at by Valery. She has a heart-stopping kind of beauty. As long as she is of this world, the atom bombs will not fall. Even the bomb will be kind to her.

Miz Literature is not bad either. But Valery Miller is an event. She moves naturally through the room. As if her beauty was an everyday occurrence. It's like having Mount Vesuvius in your own house. Beelzebub upstairs can go take a walk.

Miz Literature inspects my books.

'You don't have many women authors.'

She says it nicely, but that kind of comment can hide the most wrathful condemnation.

'I have Marguerite Yourcenar.'

Yourcenar, it seems, does not get me off the hook. Too suspect. I don't have Colette or Virginia Woolf (unforgivable!), not even Marie-Claire Blais.

'I have some Erica Jong poems.'

'Really!'

Valery's face lights up. Vesuvius in eruption. Valery illustrated a Jong collection last year. As fate would have it, the book is on the table.

Cheek to cheek in a flash-frozen tango, eyes closed, in one voice, they scream out the poem 'Sylvia Plath Is Alive in Argentine':

> *Not dead.*
> *Oh sisters, Alvarez lied....*

Miz Literature needs a little drink to go on. She pours herself a good hit of wine and it's bottoms up and the poem resumes. Valery waits like a sprinter in the blocks for the 440.

> *& she sits playing chess*
> *with Diane Arbus....*

And with raised glasses:

> *A regular girls' dormitory*
> *down there*
> *in Argentine.*

The girls are gone. I am alone in the dark. I didn't see the night close in. A crescent moon like a hat beyond the Cross. Automobile lights in the rain. Wet pavement. House lights flash on as office lights go out. I feel depressed. A kind of stylized depression.

Bouba is some specimen, lying there with his mouth wide open, and a bouquet of lilacs between his crossed arms.

A regular black dormitory, out there, with those girls!

Like a Flower Blossoming
at the End of My Black Rod

We took our last big meal before the nuclear holocaust in the
company of a girl from Sir George Williams. On the menu: white
rice, white wine and Duke. Duke Ellington. The Duke.

'I love jazz,' she jumped right in.

'Really?'

'It's so alive.'

Bouba places the pots on old copies of *National Geographic*
that were bought for that purpose at the Palais du Livre. Miz
Sophisticated Lady (that's Bouba's nickname for her, in homage
to Duke) is on a strict diet. To say she is both English and

disciplined is a needless pleonasm coming from a Negro. The wine went straight to her head. And the diet went out the window. But a half hour after the meal, I spotted her sneaking a little brown leather book from her Gucci bag.

'Are those Chairman Mao's sayings?'

'No.'

'A book of Eastern prayers?' I guessed again.

'No,' she answered sharply.

'Oh, of course! It has to be the Bhagavad-Gita.'

'You're cold.'

'In that case it's an abridged version of the Kama Sutra.'

'Sorry,' she said with a weak smile. 'It's a booklet that tells you the number of calories for different kinds of food.'

'You want to know how many carbohydrates you just ate?'

'You could put it that way,' she smiled.

'Can I see?'

She hands me the book with the same eagerness she might use to lend me her toothbrush. I go looking for an exact count of the calories and mineral salts that fill the bellies of the black world. Shrimp and rice: 402 calories. Pork fried rice: 425. Chicken fried rice: 425. We're doing all right. Rice wherever you look. I could never share the fate of a civilization that ostracizes rice. In no way could I trust people who believe yogurt is superior to rice. The taste of rice is greater than the most sublime elevations of the soul. It is one of the forms of black happiness. Black paradise found. The white (and floury) land promised since the first Slave Trade contract was signed. Is a psychoanalysis of the black soul possible? Is it not truly the dark continent? I'm asking you, Dr. Freud. Who can understand the crisis of the black who wants to become white, without losing his roots? Can you name me a single white who one fine day decided he wanted to be black? If there are any it's because of rhythm, jazz, those sparkling white teeth, the eternal suntan, the free and easy life, that high, sharp laughter. But I'm talking about a white who wants to be black just for the sake of it. I'd like to be white. Let's say I'm not totally impartial. I'd like to be a better kind of white. A white without the Oedipus complex. What good is the Oedipus complex, since you can't eat it, sell it, drink it, or trade it for a round-trip ticket to Tokyo? Or even fuck it (well, maybe so). If my wishes were granted and I suddenly turned white, what would happen? I have no idea. The question is too important for suppositions. I would see blacks in the street and know what they think when they see a white. I wouldn't want people staring at me with that covetous look in their eyes.

Bouba went out for a walk on the Mountain. It's his day out. Miz Sophisticated Lady is much better naked than I imagined. She has a wild sexuality that contrasts wonderfully with that starched look of hers. You have to be a little warped to fuck her. She got right down on all fours and I took her then and there. To my own sweet rhythm. She keeps asking for all kinds of dirty stuff and coming from Miz Sophisticated Lady, it's wonderfully perverse. I move in slow motion. A ticket to eternity. I take her from behind and she howls. High-pitched, eccentric screams. She's a nervous yet trusting fuck. It's not difficult to give her what she wants: penetrate her violently, till it hurts, then pull back nice and easy. Elementary, indeed. But surprising all the same from a Sir George girl. Looking at her tastefully dressed, you'd never suspect the voracious, insatiable little animal lodged deep in her vagina. I feel my legs tremble, the nape of my neck growing tense. The cry uncoiling deep in my stomach. The heart of my sex in jubilation like a fish swimming upstream. The Koran says, 'Is it the truth that you are preaching, or is this but a jest?' (Sura XXI, 56.) I carry her to the bed with no let-up in the rhythm, holding her at the end of my cock. Like a flower blossoming at the end of my black rod. The window still open on the Cross of Mount Royal. Miz Sophisticated Lady lying on her back. Displayed. All moist and soft. Allah be praised! This Judeo-Christian girl is my Africa. A girl born for power. So what is she doing at the end of my black rod? The juices flow between her white thighs. Her eyes are turned inward (reminding me of a childhood image of St. Thérèse of Lisieux in ecstasy). Her bent neck rests on my left shoulder. ('His left hand is under my head, and his right hand doth embrace me' – The Song of Solomon.) No sounds. Non-verbal communication. Just fucking. Fucking. Fucking. I slow the rhythm. She moans a personal Sura. I can't make out this perverse, animal esperanto. I put my ear to her mouth. 'Fuckme fuckme fuckme fuckme fuckme fuckme fuckme fuckme fuckme fuckme....' I'm coming! Let me push you over the edge. A combination of quick jabs (one two – one two three – one two) before finishing off with one from close in. Winded. She sits up suddenly then throws herself back onto the bed in a single movement as waves of spasms flow through her. I move in deep and slow. I want to fuck her subconscious. A delicate task that requires infinite control. Think about it: fucking the subconscious of a Westmount girl! I catch a glimpse of my oiled thighs (coconut oil) against this white body. I take her white breasts firmly in my hands. The light down on her white marble body. I want to fuck her identity. Pursue the racial question to the heart of her being. Are you a black man? Are you a white woman? I fuck you. You fuck me. I don't know what you're really thinking when you fuck with a black. I'd like to put you at my mercy, right here. Slow movement of the pelvis. Almost monotonous. Changes of rhythm scarcely perceptible. What about you? You're there in total metaphysical concentration and I don't know what you're thinking. But I do know there's no sexuality without fantasy. You seem unfeeling. You hardly move. Are you indifferent? Is it coming from the deepest part of your being? My sex celebrates your golden hair, your pink clitoris, your forbidden vagina, your white belly, your bowed neck, your Anglo-Saxon mouth. To touch your WASP soul. Metaphysical fucking. Mystic vapours. It's all clothed in unreality. There you are, prone, with your Ophelia face. Slowly you slip from the material world. I will pull out of this inert, unfuckable, indifferent body. I pull out slowly. What is this cry? Where does it come from? It is the cry of the vagina itself. I hear its voice: 'Yes Yes Yes Yes Yes Yes Yes Yes Yes Yes Yeeeeeeeeees.' A taut, keening cry in high C, sharp and lasting, inhuman, first allegro, then andante, then pianissimo, an endless, inconsolable, electronic asexual cry, modulation for modulation a perfect copy of the primal scream from Beelzebub's chamber above.

Duke Ellington finishes up 'Hot and Bothered.' Miz Sophisticated Lady sleeps on. I sit down to write. The Remington seems to be in a good mood. I'm typing like crazy. Clattering in the night. The sentences come all by themselves. I laugh. I'm naked. My sex still anointed. My body sweet from all the smells of Miz Sophisticated Lady. I'm writing. I'm happy and I know it.

An hour later. The middle of the night.

'Hey! Wake up!'

Miz Sophisticated Lady wakes me in the middle of the night.

'Hey!'

'What? What's wrong?'

'There are mice in here.'

I rub my eyes.

'No, there's no mice here.'

I go back to sleep.

Ten minutes later.

'Hey!'

'Now what?'

'I heard mice!'

'Oh, shit.'

'I'm sure there are mice in here.'

'In the building?'

'No, in the room.'

She is sitting in the lotus position on the bed. Neck pivoting. Her frightened eyes sweeping the room. At any moment she expects to see a single-parent family of mice come traipsing across the floor.

'I don't hear anything. Listen.'

'I heard them!'

I'm fascinated by her eyelashes flickering at an infernal rate (8,000 beats a minute, I'd say). If nothing intervenes, she'll soon enter a trance (boudham saranam gacchami) and effortlessly reach the centre of purity of Tathagata, there where no mouse may importune her.

'I'm going to go see,' she resolves.

As if it were the biggest decision of her life. I hear her switch on the bathroom light. What danger can a mouse possibly represent for a healthy Westmount girl? If a tiny mouselet sends her into panic, what about a Negro? Making love to a Negro isn't frightening; sleeping with him is. Sleep is complete surrender. It's more than nude; it's naked. Anything can happen during the night, when reason sleeps. Do we dream our lover? Do we penetrate his dreams? Shifting sands, says the Western world. Danger. Beware. Danger of osmosis. Danger of true communication. What started out as a simple roll in the hay can turn into.... It's happened before: young, white, Protestant Anglo-Saxon girls sleep with a Negro and wake up under a baobab tree in the middle of the bush, talking over family affairs with the village women. Did you hear about the daughter of one of the heads of Canadian Pacific who lay down with a Negro on Mount Royal one summer's day, in plain sight? No one's seen her since. And the daughter of the program director at Radio-Canada is selling reed baskets and fishing nets in a little Casamance village. What about the wife of one of the members of the McGill board of directors who's harvesting peanuts in Senegal? There's no end to cases like this. Be careful. Fucking with a Negro is all right (it's even recommended), but sleeping with one.... I picture Miz Sophisticated Lady running down an antelope, preparing manioc to make cassava and serving tea at the death-bed vigil. 'Sleep with a Negro and wake up in Togoland' – a new travel agent ad. What is Miz Sophisticated Lady doing in the dark with this Negro? Chasing after a mouse. I fall back asleep, battle-weary, leaving her to the hunt. Gently, I enter sleep. In slow-motion flight. I clearly hear Duke Ellington playing 'The Soda Fountain Rag.' The rag reminds Duke of the good old days at the Poodle Dog Café. Duke plays this hilarious thing with guys who can crack you up. Edison and Cootie Williams on clarinet (who could ask for more?), Bubber Miley and Stewart blowing trumpet with a disdainful sound as if their minds were somewhere else, but how it swings! Al Sears, Al the Great, on sax. Brand on bass (can't you just hear it?) and Sonny Greer on drums. With a band like that you could bring down the house. Upstairs, Beelzebub is sleeping. Hades in repose.

'Hey!'

'Hey' is for horses! Don't these Westmount girls have any couth? They don't respect the sleep of their bedmates. Miz Sophisticated Lady, it seems, has stumbled onto something.

That something is Bouba. Bouba sitting on the couch in the darkness, devouring a head of lettuce. (The Koran says, 'You shall eat the fruit of the Zaqqum-tree' – Sura LVI, 52 – 'and fruits of your own choice and the flesh of fowls that you relish' – Sura LVI, 28.) I must admit it's an impressive sight for a Westmount girl. I didn't hear Bouba come in. He must have been quiet about it. And since Bouba eats anything at any hour of the day, he must have opened the fridge with a hole in his stomach, only to find a head of lettuce. He must have set about consuming it in silence. But Miz Sophisticated Lady's sharp ears picked up the sound of gnawing incisors. And now she has come upon Bouba devouring a head of lettuce in the dark.

'I don't get it,' was her only comment.

She does not get it.

'It's not easy.'

'I just can't understand such a thing.'

She just cannot understand such a thing.

'It's just that way.'

'Can't you explain it?'

'Can it wait till tomorrow?'

As if I had refused a drowning man a life preserver. How can I tell her that this cultivated, concerned young man with whom she chatted away the afternoon nourishes in his heart of hearts a deep and abiding hatred of milk, steak, cheese and eggs? ('Believers, do not forbid the wholesome things which Allah has made lawful to you.' Sura V, 89.) Would she believe me? Or at least understand? It goes back to the embryonic stage of the black man. For Bouba, these foods are and will forever be malevolent devils working to reduce him to slavery. Bouba is a brave man engaged in constant warfare in his very chamber. Warring against dark forces of blackest despair. He knows he doesn't stand a chance. His body is covered with scars. Wounds, some still bleeding. Blows that would prove mortal for most. But every night (and tonight was no exception) he continues to match swords in hand-to-hand combat with the hydra of the Stomach.

I really laid it on thick. And immediately regretted trying to explain this very private combat to a girl from Sir George who's been following the Scarsdale diet since her first period. She told me that the Self must have another destiny than to gulp down carbohydrates. For a famished Negro, Hegelian man is one of the sickest jokes in the Judeo-Christian panoply.

The Cotton Club Orchestra launches into 'Mood Indigo.' I hear Bouba whistling in the dark. Miz Sophisticated Lady is sitting on the bed in the higher biped position. Upright, proud, pathetic. Miz S.L. is literally bursting with indignation. I don't know exactly when I committed the fatal faux pas. But it was monumental. Irreparable. It must have been when I said that Negroes are still at the Big Feed stage and that for them eating a bowl of rice is sometimes preferable to the mysteries of love. Normally, the Negro should be upset, indignant at still being in such a terrible situation. There's no reason for an English girl to get upset. Besides, comparing a Westmount girl to a bowl of rice is a philosophical reflection beyond my means. Mao did not make the revolution so that every Chinaman could enjoy a Chinawoman, but so that every Chinaman and Chinawoman could enjoy a bowl of rice a day. Therefore, for the Chinese, man or woman, rice is a sacred thing. Whereas for Miz Sophisticated Lady, a bowl of rice is a bowl of rice. She won't let me call a cab. The pride of the powerful. She exits. And the more I think about it, the more I believe that it really wasn't a fight over rice, but an old historical misunderstanding, irreparable, total and definitive, a misunderstanding over race, caste, class, sex, nation and religion.

In the hollow of his palm, Bouba assembles the frail chicken bones that were lying on the table. I settle in on the couch with Borges and thirty seconds later the first notes of 'Take the A Train' fill the room. The music insinuates itself into my sinews, casting me into that moist, tropical sound jungle as old Duke looks on with cool, ironic eyes. While Bouba keeps time with two Chinese chopsticks.

'Hear that, man?'

'I hear it.'

'"Hot and Bothered" – you like that?'

'It's okay.'

'Admit it's genius, admit you've never heard anything like that in your whole lousy life.'

'I admit.'

'And *there*,' Bouba goes on. 'Stravinsky took the line and ran with it.'

'What's that?'

'You didn't recognize it?'

'No.'

'"Sophisticated Lady," man. Pure symphonic jazz.'

Negroes at the Exile Café

Bistrot à Jojo. Noon. Warm temperature.

We're sitting at the back. In the shadow of filtered light. Armchairs. Soft soundtrack. A bar for the well-off.

We order zombies.

The man across from me is from the Ivory Coast. He's been in Montreal fifteen years. He went through the October Crisis.

'What was it like?'

'You mean October?'

'I'm not talking about that.'

'You mean the "decline."'

'That's right.'

He takes a lungful of air.

'You know something, brother, there was a time when black meant something here. We picked up girls just like that.'

He snaps his fingers. A black angel moves across the field.

He looks at me with his parchment face, a delirious sage under a baobab tree on a full-moon night.

'Yes, brother, it was the golden age of black.'

The ivory age, I'd say.

The waiter finally arrives with our drinks. A big tip.

'The tip is very important, brother. It's your respect, your dignity, your survival.'

The man is totally disillusioned. As if he had let go a long time ago. And been falling ever since. Free fall.

I get things going again.

'What percentage?'

'You mean the tip?'

'No, the girls.'

'One black for six white girls. And there, brother, I'm talking about your average black man of average height and appetite. In the smaller towns, we were king of the castle. Those were the good old days, brother, if ever there were any.'

A tall Senegalese (six feet six) walks across the café to our table.

'Brothers.'

'Hello, brother.'

Another round. Three beers this time. The Senegalese is as tall and thin as a bamboo stalk in his dashiki.

He sits down.

A long silence.

We drink. Another round. Three more beers.

'How many do I have?'

'Two, like the rest of us.'

'Don't take me for that kind, brother.'

He shows me a tuft of white hair in the middle of his head like a cockade.

'How many?' he asks again.

I still don't understand.

The Ivory Coast man emerges from his silence to translate for me.

'He wants to know how many winters you think he's spent here.'

'Ten,' I say to avoid offending him.

He bursts out laughing.

'Exactly twenty, brother. We're burned up inside. Ice burns up everything here, brother. After twenty years here, you turn into ash. Look at that guy coming in. Looks hearty, doesn't he? A strong wind will blow him over.'

The newcomer does look a little wind-blown. And furious too. He sits down and orders a beer and a pack of Gitanes.

'You know,' he says after listening to our conversation a while, 'I can't stand this talk about white girls any more.'

'What happened to you?'

'We blacks need to be left alone,' he declares.

'Of course,' I say.

Everyone nods his head.

'You can love me or you can spit on me,' he continues. 'I couldn't care less. It's all the same to me. The same hypocritical bullshit. I'm fed up, brothers, fed up.'

A respectful silence. The man drinks from his beer and shakes his head. He smiles sadly.

'I met a girl here once, in this very bar. We drink together. We go to another place. I live near here. You know, the classic progression. I bring her to my place. Two days I'll never forget. She eats spicy – very good. She fucks hard – even better. Everything's fine. Smooth as silk. I let her leave. I have to, right? She's supposed to go canoeing with her family. I like people who have a sense of family. She swears she loves no one but me. I didn't ask her to say that. She leaves. Not even a call. Nothing. I'm still waiting. Not a word. Three months later I meet her on St. Denis. "Hello, there." "Oh, hello," she says. "Why didn't you call?" She couldn't. Didn't have time. Three months and no time to call. When I think of what that girl said to me when we were fucking. "And what have you been doing all this time?" "I learned to play the congas. With a marvellous teacher. Maybe you know him. He's a wise man. He's taught me all kinds of secrets. His throne is a couch, and he lies down on it. He's the greatest sage in Montreal."'

After his confession, the man stares at me with his little razor-blade eyes. I know that sage who lives on a couch, but I never suspected his reputation had gone beyond the borders of the Carré St. Louis.

A Young Black Montreal Writer
Puts James Baldwin out to Pasture

The bouquet of peonies sleeps by the old Remington. A lousy
Sunday. Ashen, grey and damp. I feel empty. Horizontal on the
couch, Bouba is drinking hot tea. Ella Fitzgerald's soft voice
singing 'Lullaby of Birdland.'
   'You don't look too good, man.'
   'I'm all right,' I say in a small voice.
   'You don't convince me.'
   'I'm not trying to.'
   'You want a cup?'
   'Okay.'

The hot tea is good.

'It's because of the book?'

'I guess so....'

'That's why.'

'I'm stuck. I'm not getting anywhere.'

'You should go out for a walk.'

'That's the tenth time you've given me that piece of advice.'

'You know what, man?'

'What?'

'I've been meaning to tell you. Your problem is you think too much.'

'I know.'

In a voice that makes you feel like you've got a rope around your neck, Billie Holiday sings 'Strange Fruit.' The song gives me a desperate case of the blues.

Miz Literature comes in and stands behind my chair.

'Are you going to keep on working?'

'Maybe.'

'Do you think you'll get somewhere?'

'I don't know.'

'If there's some way I could help you....'

'Unfortunately, it's the kind of thing you have to do yourself.'

Miz Literature comes back to observe a half-hour later.

'Cool, brother!'

'Since when do Outremont girls talk like that?'

'Since they hang out with blacks.'

'Be specific – since they go to bed with blacks.'

'You're young, gifted and black, is that it?'

'And you're just rich, is that it?'

'Not just rich, since I'm going to bed with a young, gifted black.'

'You trying to ruin your Outremont reputation?'

'What have you got against the rich?'

'What do I have against the rich? I'm green with envy, I'm yellow with jealousy. I want to be rich and famous.'

'You realize I'm taking you seriously.'

'Good. That's the only serious thing I've said in months.'

'You want to become the best black writer?'

'That's right. Better than Dick Wright.'

'Better than Chester Himes?'

'Better than Chester.'

'Better than James Baldwin?'

'Baldwin's all worn out!'

'Better than Baldwin or not?'

'Better than Baldwin. "With *Black Cruiser's Paradise*, a young black Montreal writer puts James Baldwin out to pasture."'

The rain stopped a while ago. It's stifling in here.

'Why don't we go out?'

'Where to?'

'Outside.'

'It's no better out there.'

'It's different.'

'You want a change of scene?'

'That's about it.'

It stinks in here, but Miz Literature can put up with the smell better than I can.

'It's hot, huh?'

'Very hot.'

'How hot is it?'

'Ninety or thereabouts.'

'Look at that bike.'

'Which one? Down there?'

'Watch carefully.'

'Why?'

'It's going to evaporate before it reaches St. Catherine.'

'Are you crazy? What are you talking about?'

'Just watch.'

'Oh no!'

'I told you so.'

'Oh, my God! My God! My God!'

'Are you going to say that all day?'

'Oh, my God!'

We go into Hachette. Artificial cool. The bookstore's full.

'Look at the crowd!'

'It's because of the air conditioning. Most of them don't have the slightest intention of buying a book. They're here for the cool air.'

'What are they reading?'

'Cookbooks, macrame, diet, horoscope, great outdoors, sports. Stanké and his gang.'

'What are we going to read?'

'We're here to steal. When you rip off a book, you must choose only the best. When I want to read a bad book, I buy it. Getting caught with a lousy writer under your shirt is the greatest humiliation.'

'What are we going to steal?'

'Suit yourself.'

I've got the cashier all figured out. She looks but she doesn't see. Better pay attention to the guy standing with his hands behind his back, near the paperbacks. He's the floorwalker.

Miz Literature is whispering away. That's her way of panicking.

'Keep your eyes open for ladies in their sixties – you know, flower-print dresses, silver hair, clean hands, Madame Respectable. They're liable to squeal on you just to get in good with the store manager. That gives them legitimacy, since they come here every day.'

Miz Literature is all hot and bothered. The biggest adventure in her life. Theft. Corrupting an Outremont girl is practically a BA in itself.

'How many do you have in your bag?'

'Five or six, I don't know.'

'That's a day's work. Let's go. Give me your bag. Go ahead, I'll follow. Don't look at the cashier. I'll take care of everything.'

Miz Literature is in exultation.

'You know, I made a wish back there.'

'What's that?'

'One day we'll come here and steal your book.'

I close my eyes. And picture, with a dash of perverse pleasure, an old lady slipping a book unnoticed into her purse: *Black Cruiser's Paradise*.

Miz Clockwork Orange's Electronic Rhythm Drowning out Black Congas

I turn onto St. Catherine Street.
'Hello, Black Beauty.'
A transvestite.
'Where's the Clochards Célèstes?'
'That way, Beautiful.'
Bouba left me a message next to the Remington. Miz Literature had come by at noon. She'd be waiting for me tonight at the Clochards Célèstes.
The staircase is as narrow as a rope ladder. Two spacious rooms. A bar. A trio of guys in battered fedoras, elbows on the

bar, watching a baseball game on TV. No sound. The TV is on a shelf next to an enormous Budweiser bottle. This Bud's for you.

'A Bud.'

Advertising works.

At the far end of the room, thirty tables around a stage. Senegalese playing music. Four drums, two congas. Insistent, frenetic rhythm. Zoom to the back, right: Miz Literature sipping something green. Electricity in the air. The black bodies of the Senegalese glow in the darkness shot through with magnesium flashes. A whiff of hashish, light but persistent. I cross the room through the Senegalese show. The moist pulse of burnt bodies waiting for a rain of nago rhythm. Call of the bush on St. Catherine Street. Black music for white dancers. Soul. Soul on fire. High tension. Miz Literature is talking with a punk girl. Miz Punk shoots me a killing glance. She wants to play rough.

Koko, one of the Senegalese musicians, winks my way. *Brother.* Miz Punk caught the signal.

'Where are you from?'

'Harlem.'

'Harlem! I love Harlem.'

'Do you?'

Miz Punk is totally wired.

'Is there a lot of crime?'

'You do what you can.'

'I heard no one makes it past seventeen. You die first. Is that true?'

'Sure. I'm fifteen myself.'

Miz Punk is seventeen. She gives me a strange look, trying to ferret out the famous Harlem beat in me. The killer instinct. I shake my head gently with my best Malcolm X look.

The Senegalese finish their show in a burst of frenzied rhythm. They gather up their instruments (drums, congas, kora), wave goodbye and go headlong down the suicide stairway, followed by a cluster of dashiki-clad groupies. Colonialized white girls. The priestesses of the Temple of Race. High on Negro.

The DJ puts on hard rock. Miz Punk leaps onto the dance floor. Tina Turner. She starts jumping up and down. Madness. Dervish. Hard face, upper lip split by a razor slash, deep-set eyes, her body dislocated, disjointed, off-centre, fragmented. She dances a half-hour with no reprieve. Miz Punk lasts longer than the copper-top battery. ('You, as well as they, are doomed to die.' Sura XXXIX, 31.)

We don't waste time getting out of there, Miz Literature and I, leaving Miz Punk, alias Miz Clockwork Orange, to crash through the floor of the Clochards Célestes. It's raining. We take shelter under the marquee of the Théâtre du Nouveau Monde. Miz Literature kisses me on the mouth in front of the *Death of a Salesman* poster. We take the 129. Miz Literature has wet hair, which only adds to her charm.

'I don't want any unpleasant surprises.'

'I'm telling you for the hundredth time, my parents are in Europe. I got a telegram this morning. Here's the proof.'

She rummages through her bag and pulls out a balled-up piece of paper. Then wipes off her lipstick with it and throws it away, into the rain.

Her room is upstairs, across from her younger sister's (a Roy Orbison groupie). Posters of Roy everywhere. Roy at the National Arts Centre. She pinned a tiny photo on the picture of Roy that covers the whole left side of the room: two sun-tanned girls hitch-hiking with their tops off. Roy at the Peterborough Memorial Centre, with a certain Vicky. Roy at the Lord Beaverbrook (this time she wrote 'Roy Roy Roy' on the poster in black felt-tip pen). Roy at Toronto's Massey Hall and the Winnipeg Concert Hall (consumption in the hall that night: one ton of marijuana). The last concert was on Vicky's sixteenth birthday. On a Roy poster she scrawled in eyebrow pencil, 'I just feel like killing myself.'

'Those are Penny's things, she's my younger sister. She's really crazy. She's on tour now with Men at Work.'

Miz Literature puts on a Simon and Garfunkel record and runs off to the bathroom to dry her hair. I stay in her room. Cushions everywhere. All kinds of colours. Left-over from the sit-in days of the seventies. Books piled up on the floor next to an old Telefunken record player. To the left, facing the door, a large walnut wardrobe. Reproductions: a beautiful Brueghel. An Utamaro by the window. A splendid Piranese, two Hokusai prints and in the corner by the library (made of bricks and boards) a precious Holbein. By her bedside, against the pink wall, Miz Literature placed a large photo of Virginia Woolf taken in 1939 by Gisèle Freud at Monk House, Rodwell, Sussex.

I can hear the water running in the bathroom sink. Private sounds. A wet body. The luxury of soft Anglo-Saxon intimacy. Big red-brick house with walls scaled by ivy. English lawn. Victorian calm. Deep armchairs. Old daguerreotypes. The patina of antiques. Shiny black piano. Engravings from another age. Group portrait with corgis. Bankers (double chin and monocle) playing cricket. Portraits of young girls with long, fine, sickly features. Diplomat in pith helmet posted to New Delhi. Odour of Calcutta. This house breathes calm, tranquillity, order. The order of the pillagers of Africa. Britannia rules the waves. Everything here has its place – except me. I'm here for the sole purpose of fucking the daughter. Therefore, I too have my place. I'm here to fuck the daughter of these haughty diplomats who once whacked us with their sticks. I wasn't there at the time of course, but what do you want, history hasn't been good to us, but we can always use it as an aphrodisiac.

Miz Literature walks into the room. Tired but still smiling. I'm lucky to have found her.
    'Sherry?'
    'Sherry.'
    'What would you like to hear?'
    'Furey.'
    'Sherry with Furey.'

A Description of My Room at 3670 Rue St-Denis

Bessie Smith (1896-1937), Chattanooga, Tennessee. Poor Bessie. I'm so down-hearted, heart-broken too. I'm stretched out on the river bottom ('Mississippi Floods'), with the songs of the cotton pickers for a lullaby. The Mississippi invented the blues. Every note holds a drop of water. A drop of Bessie's blood. 'When it rained five days and the sky turned black as night / When it thundered and lightninged and the wind began to blow....'

Poor Bessie. Poor Mississippi. Poor muddy-water girl. Poor Bessie with her lynched heart. Black bodies running with sweat, bent over the snowy grace of the cotton. Black bodies shining sensual, beaten by the cruel wind of the Deep South. Two hundred years of desire thrown together, boxed in, piled up and sent down the Mississippi in the hold of a riverboat. Black desire obsessed with pubescent white flesh. Desire reined in like a mad dog. Desire flaming up. Desire for the white woman.

'What's happening to you, man?'

'What do you mean?'

'You're afraid?'

'Afraid of what?'

'Afraid of the goddamn blank page?'

'That's it.'

'Squeeze it, man, grab it and make it cry for mercy, humanize your goddamn blank page.'

A description of my room at 3670 rue St-Denis (done in cooperation with my old Remington 22).

I write: bed.

I see: dank mattress, dirty sheet, pounded-out pillow, corrugated couch.

I think: sleep (Bouba sleeps twelve hours straight), make love (Miz Sophisticated Lady), daydream in bed (with Miz Literature), write in bed (*Black Cruiser's Paradise*), read in bed (Miller, Cendrars, Bukowski).

Miller, Cendrars, Bukowski.

I must be dreaming.

I'm sitting by myself on a bench in the Carré St. Louis. There's a guy sitting across from me; I look without really seeing him. Something about him catches my eye. I know that guy. I'm sure I've seen his face somewhere. Where the hell could it have been? That long, full, refined face – I know it. I don't know why I can't place him. Slightly hooded eyes, completely bald, face like a bonze monk – holy shit, it's Miller. Henry Miller. Henry Miller in the Carré St. Louis! I can't believe my eyes. Miller sitting sipping on a Molson. Just like that. Henry Miller. Miller, the old sod. Incredible. I must be dreaming. A hallucination. The effects of hunger. I pinch myself. He's still there. Miller himself. That hungry mouth ready for the finest morsels. He's talking to a guy

next to him. A bum. Maybe not. Shit ... it's Cendrars. Blaise
Cendrars. The one-armed man. I must be completely nuts.
Miller and Cendrars in the Carré St. Louis. Right next to me. I
move closer. They'll disappear in a puff of smoke. The genie
back in its bottle. They're still there, talking away, minding their
own business. I can actually touch them.

'Slide over, Miller,' I tell him.

Cendrars looks over at me.

'How're you doing, Blaise?'

Police sirens. The cops pick up a guy who's all bloody. It's
Bukowski.

Bukowski in deep shit again!

'Wake up, man. You've been sleeping on the machine for an
hour. You won't be able to straighten out your neck.'

'An hour!'

'My watch never lies, man.'

'You mean it was just a dream?'

'What dream?'

'It was totally crazy. I dreamed I was talking with – you'll
never guess who.'

'Miller, Cendrars and Bukowski.'

'Shit! How'd you know?'

'What do you mean how'd I know? It's all written right here
in black and white. Who else would have written that?'

'Written what?'

'Written this passage. There's two of us here, right? You and
me. So who wrote it? Your Remington?'

'Could be. It could have been my Remington, Bouba. Don't
forget the machine belonged to Chester Himes.'

'You need a little rest, man.'

New description of my room at 3670 rue St-Denis (done in
cooperation with my Remington 22).

I write: toilet.

I see: two dirty towels, three bars of soap, one after-shave, two
bandages, two toothbrushes, one deodorant stick (English
Leather), two tubes of Colgate toothpaste, one jar of Alka Seltzer,
one electric razor (gift from Miz Literature), two bottles of

Astring-o-Sol; one box of Q-Tips, a dozen Shields condoms (extra sensitive, contoured for better fit, lubricated), one box of Kotex (left behind by a Toronto girl, Miz Security), a bottle of cologne and a jar of aspirin.

I think: read Salinger in a steambath with Miz Literature and make love in the shower with Miz Sophisticated Lady.

I write: refrigerator.

I see: one bottle of water, one half-empty can of tomato paste, one three-quarters-empty jar of relish, a big hunk of oka cheese, two bottles of beer and a bag of carrots.

I write: window.

I see that lousy cross framed in my window.

I write: alcohol lamp.

I see Miz Suicide and Bouba talking in hushed voices, drinking Shanghai tea.

I write: couch.

I see the old couch where Bouba reads Freud as he listens to jazz all day.

I write: jazz.

I listen to Coltrane, Parker, Ellington, Fitzgerald, Smith, Holiday, Art Tatum, Miles Davis, B. B. King, Bix Biederbecke, Jelly Roll Morton, Armstrong, T. S. Monk, Fats Waller, Lester Young, John Lee Hooker, Coleman Hawkins and Cosy Cole.

I write: box of books.

I read: Hemingway, Miller, Cendrars, Bukowski, Freud, Proust, Cervantes, Borges, Cortazar, Dos Passos, Mishima, Apollinaire, Ducharme, Cohen, Villon, Lévy-Beaulieu, Fennario, Himes, Baldwin, Wright, Pavese, Aquin, Quevedo, Ousmane, J.-S. Alexis, Roumain, G. Roy, De Quincey, Marquez, Jong, Alejo Carpentier, Atwood, Asturias, Amado, Fuentes, Kerouac, Corso, Handke, Limonov, Yourcenar.

I write: typewriter.

I see my old Remington 22 typing this.

Miz Snob Plays a Tune
from *India Song*

I'm sitting outside at the Faubourg St-Denis, sipping a glass of cheap wine and watching the girls go by. A girl to my right is reading something by Miller. I lean over to see which one. One of my favourites: *Quiet Days in Clichy.* Miller's summer in Paris. You have to read Miller in the summer and Ducharme in the winter, alone in a cottage. Wouldn't you know it: here comes a girl carrying Ducharme's *L'hiver de force*, that's just come out with Gallimard. It's the hottest book around. It's like the summer when Capote published *Breakfast at Tiffany's;* every waiter in Manhattan had a copy.

Miz Literature is waiting for me at the Beaux Esprits, a dim bar decorated with exotic plants. Rhododendrons (black foliage with pink flares), saxifragaceae, cacti, agapanthus, zingiberaceae, cactaceae. Uproarious growth. You practically need a machete to cut your way through.

I take a look around. The bar is almost deserted. A pair of eccentric girls smoking Egyptian cigarettes are chatting away near the entrance.

'Where do you come from?' the girl with Miz Literature wants to know.

Every time I'm asked that question, flat out like that, without any previous *National Geographic* references, an irresistible desire to kill fills me. The girl is wearing a tweed skirt complemented by a white blouse in some refined material. No doubt about it, she's a snob. Miz Snob.

'What country do you come from?' she asks me again.

'On Thursday evenings I come from Madagascar.'

The waiter appears. Blond hair and Botticelli face.

'A sherry for me,' Miz Snob announces.

A kir for Miz Literature.

'I'll have a screwdriver.'

If you want to be treated with a minimum of respect in a place like this, avoid ordering a beer at all costs.

The barman is done up in the latest fashion. He paces from one end of the bar to the other, a good seven meters at least. His pale face in continual movement like a mechanical doll against a red-brick background. Mechanical Doll dives below the bar like an oyster fisherman, brings up the orange juice and pours it into a tall glass (with one-quarter vodka), the entire process taking eight and three-tenths seconds. As two Benin masks look on impassively.

Marguerite Duras is at the Cinémathèque this week. Miz Snob took in two films this afternoon.

'Have you seen *India Song?*' Miz Literature asks me.

'A superb film,' Miz Snob answers for me.

We gaze into our respective glasses. Five minutes later, Miz Literature stages a comeback. She wants to show Miz Snob that her boyfriend is not a cultural wash-out.

'Have you seen *Hiroshima, Mon Amour?*' she asks me pointedly.

'No,' I tell her.

There you go. This Negro is a cultural wash-out.

'Just some of the rushes,' I add out of pity for Miz Literature.

'You saw the rushes?' Miz Snob bellows.

With a mixture of 48% ex-hippie, 12% Black Panther, 9.5% blasé and 0.5% sexy, I let on, 'Patrick Straram *le bison ravi* organized a private screening the last time M.D. was in town.'

'You spoke to her?'

'To whom?'

'You spoke to Marguerite Duras?'

These McGill girls are totally lacking in tact.

'Not really. We chatted about *India Song* a little.'

'What did she say?'

'What you'd expect her to say in a case like that.'

'What did she tell you about *India Song*?'

'Well ... it's hard to remember what you said and what people said to you at a party.'

'You spoke to Marguerite Duras! You must remember what she said to you.'

'If you really must know, we talked about the problems she was having with the editing.'

'What type of problems?'

'If I remember right – I'd had a little bit to drink, I don't know if you've ever been to a party at Straram's – anyway, I think she was having problems with the soundtrack. In the end she took the soundtrack from another film and edited it onto *India Song*. I think it was from a documentary, that's right, a documentary on Hokusai.'

And when you consider that these girls were sent to a serious institution like McGill to learn clarity of thought, analytical capacity and scientific doubt! But they're so full of Judeo-Christian propaganda that when they get around a Negro, they immediately start thinking like primitives. For them, a Negro is too naïve to lie. But they didn't start the ball rolling; before them was the Bible, Rousseau, the blues, Hollywood and all the rest.

Miz Snob invites us back for tea at her house. Miz Literature doesn't have a car; Miz Snob has an MG. She lives next to the Outremont Cinema. Tree-lined streets. Near St. Viateur. French butcher shop. Greek pastry shop. Bookstore close by.

Miz Snob shares a seven-and-a-half with two other McGill girls who are out at Jasper for the summer. A large living and dining room, a spacious kitchen, three small bedrooms. One window facing west and two east. A nice bathroom with an antique tub. An antique mirror on the shiny black wall. In front of her bedroom window, Miz Snob has a big walnut bed that forms an angle with a large armoire. A black piano against a high-gloss white wall. An old daguerreotype under a soft spotlight (gift from her grandmother, Toronto's first woman photographer).

Miz Snob is studying photography at McGill. According to the posters in the big living room, Henri Cartier-Bresson and Marguerite Duras are the only citizens of this planet. I must admit, Miz Snob is sexier than M.D. She uses a professional Nikon model and used to go out with a Japanese guy during her Dawson College days.

A room with bright stained-glass panels, like the Bibliothèque Nationale on St. Denis. They remind you of children's drawings. A Chagall reproduction hanging on the wall. Chagall shines. In the centre of the drawing, an enormous circle with eight spheres of Mozartian clarity. All around, fish, birds, earthly animals and letters of the alphabet dance a joyful round watched over by the Lion of Judah (a young lion with round, domesticated paws). In the distance: Jerusalem, the yellow city.

Miz Literature disappeared into an album of Lewis Hine's photographs when we got here and hasn't been seen from since.

The steaming tea is served in a handsome Dresden china service. Another gift from the Toronto grandmother. I assume the Black Cat position on the hassock. Incense wafts toward the ceiling. Great clouds, like Sioux signals. I watch them float upward and feel myself about to launch into a gustatory description, mingling the delectation of the spices of the Sugar Route with the seven savours of ginger at the noon hour, ending with a dazzling leap (the new black Malraux) whereby the Tao would dissolve in this Dresden china teapot – but no one would forgive me for that.

Miz Literature is completely wiped out. She goes to lie down

in one of the empty rooms. Miz Snob, so I understand, is
insomniac. Now we are alone.

Miz Snob goes to the kitchen for more tea. I feel as soft as one
of those Rocky Mountain land crabs. I surrender to my daquiri.
Half horizontal on a hassock, I carry out a lascivious inspection
of the room: the sculpted wood of antique furniture; a flea
market chair; Polynesian seashells around a Dahomey sculpture
on a tiny shelf; two batiks of New Delhi women in light silk saris
standing on the right bank of the Ganges.

And snobbishly floating in the air from a chain, an enormous
Truman Capote portrait (with hat) shot by Andy Warhol.

Miz Snob suddenly reappears with hot tea and catches me
rummaging in her records.

'Do you like Cohen?'

Since no one ever mentions Cohen without saying something
about Dylan in the next breath, I follow the pattern.

'I prefer him to Dylan. His early songs, at least.'

Miz Snob almost spilled my daquiri. She likes Cohen, but
Dylan is king.

That wry guitar always creates a special mood. Sinking into a
hassock, listening to Cohen, drinking Shanghai tea.

Miz Snob searches for Rampal among her records. She kneels
down. I assure you she is wearing a tiny white satin
undergarment. Her body is white, untouched, smooth, almost
shiny.

'Are you hungry?' she asks me out of nowhere.

'A little.'

'I'm going to make an omelette.'

I follow her into the clean, well-lighted kitchen. Handsome
pale wood, big farmhouse table and a collection of spice bottles
(thyme, dried nutmeg, curry, paprika, sage, mustard, chives,
parsley) above an Arcimboldo poster of a man's head with a
collage of fruits of the sea and land. On a shelf in a corner: a
collection of *Time-Life* recipe books.

Miz Snob attends to her omelette. She breaks the eggs with a
sharp tap against the edge of the pan. I watch her
shoulderblades moving under her tight white blouse. Muscles.
Not an ounce of fat. A Scarsdale girl. But her breasts, that should

be smaller, are big enough to stand out on both sides. I'm standing behind her. Of its own accord, my hand pops from my pocket, where it lay in repose like an extinct volcano, and sweeps around her waist that conjures up Jane Birkin's curves. I bend over and kiss her pointy ear. That wasn't the thing to do. She didn't slap me, nothing like that. It was worse. She and I – really, it was she – decided we weren't going to be great lovers.

Miz Snob sprinkles cocaine on the omelette. She puts some in everything she eats. She's crazy about coke.

Coke and I are not the best of friends.

We talk about Hölderlin, that old madman, with Rampal providing the background. Très snob, man.

'Have you read Burroughs?'

'Yes. But when it comes to the Beats, I prefer Corso.'

Excellent Colombian stock. Too bad it's wasted on me.

'Did you like *Junkie?*'

Name-dropping 101: Miz Snob's favourite subject.

'It was all right. I liked *Naked Lunch* better.'

'I thought it was too obvious. It can't stand up next to De Quincey's *Journal.*'

Rampal, when it comes down to it, is a lot of crap. You can keep him. But Miz Snob has a good pusher.

Hats off, Colombia. White satin. Black pain.

Miz Mystic Flying back from Tibet

As I climb the stairway I hear old Mingus playing. Charles
Mingus, if you please. The door is slightly ajar. I push it and
walk in. Miz Suicide is sitting at Bouba's feet in the lotus
position. Black Buddha is devouring an enormous pizza. Miz
Suicide is with a girl who just came back from Tibet. Miz Mystic.
Miz Mystic is a carbon copy of an iguana. Bouba's bestiary. Eyes
unfocused, body redundant, Miz Mystic is in a constant state of
flotation. To keep from surrendering my vital energies to these
monsters, I leap upon the last piece of pizza. Fortune has saved
me a few dregs of wine in the bottle. As usual, Miz Suicide is

busy boiling water for tea. I sit down on my work chair, turn my back on the typewriter and gaze stupidly on that lousy cross that haunts my window. Miz Suicide serves tea. Miz Mystic floats. Bouba reads suras to jazz rhythm. Miz Mystic is unapproachable.

'What's Tibet like?'

'It's okay.'

'Just okay? That's all? I thought a trip to Tibet would be something special.'

She ignores me.

'Do they levitate mountains over there?'

A frigid look.

'I didn't see any of that.'

'I don't know, I figure some incredible things must go on in those frozen caves.'

'Not especially.'

Miz Mystic sits with her back against the Japanese screen. Her eyes are like those of a lama contemplating an edelweiss. Miz Suicide is working on her third tea. Mingus launches into a capricious piece that makes a crazy contrast with this mystico-depressing scene. Bouba is lying on the couch like the Dalai Lama of the Carré St. Louis. The fatigue of two sleepless nights is beginning to hit me. This planet is not going well at all. ('Dhul-Qarnain,' they said, 'Gog and Magog are ravaging this land. Build us a rampart against them and we will pay you tribute.') I formulate this vow, then fall into a cotton-wool sleep, diagonally across the bed. As Mingus plays 'Goodbye Pork Pie Hat.'

I wake up with a start to see Miz Mystic psychotically pounding the bed. Then she makes a dash for the window and tries to jump out. Bouba grabs her by the waist. Miz Suicide has a hold on her foot. The insensitive needle scratches at the record. Miz Mystic is foaming with held-back rage. Her desire to throw herself out the window is so strong it seems legitimate to me. In cases of great conviction, we should make an exception. Let her do it. Someone wants to kill himself. So be it. ('Say: Nothing will your flight avail you. If you escaped from death and slaughter you would enjoy this world only for a little while.') Miz Mystic has her torso out the window. Her skirt is pushed up to her waist. Dry, bare legs. Miz Suicide pulls her back desperately. Miz

Mystic is making good headway toward the void as the indifferent cross looks on.

When it occurs to me what is going on, I get up. Bouba and Miz Suicide help me pull Miz Mystic back inside.

Miz Mystic is sleeping now on the couch. A crescent moon like a hat beyond the cross. The Remington glows in the dark. Solemnly, Charles Mingus attacks 'The Pithecanthropus Erectus' (1956). By the pizza box, in the middle of the room, one of Miz Mystic's shoes. I can see the filigree of scrapes and scratches on the heel. Suddenly, I'm depressed. This room is the headquarters for every marginal character in town. The urban mafia of crazies instinctively turns to 3670 rue St-Denis, off the Carré St. Louis, Montreal, Quebec, Canada, America, Earth. My house. Will this honest, conscientious black cruise artist never find his paradise? I want Carole Laure! I demand Carole Laure! Bring me Carole Laure!

The Black Poet Dreams of Buggering an Old Stalinist on the Nevsky Prospect

It's horribly hot. The Carré St. Louis is full of bare-chested drunkards. The sticky air stinks of beer. Upstairs in the room we're roasting. It's hell, I'm telling you. Reason enough to go downstairs. Only Beelzebub could fuck in this heat. His moaning bugs me. Fire must be shooting out of his mouth up there.

The Carré St. Louis is not your average place. That mossy ground. All the filthy brats you could ask for. A girl photographing Pauline Julien's house.

A bum comes up for a hand-out.

'Got any spare change?'

'No.'

'That's all right, I'll tell you anyway.'

He takes a tiny scrap of paper out of his pocket.

'Look. What do you see?'

'A map of Africa cut out from *Time* magazine.'

He looks me in the eye.

'You're right,' he says. 'How did you know?'

'It says so under the map.'

'Oh, you're an intellectual!'

'I know how to read. And how to use my fists too.'

He raises his left hand to show he doesn't want trouble.

'All right, all right. Show me your country on the map.'

'Ivory Coast. Right there.'

I point to the first country I can make out.

'Ivory Coast! Is that where you're from? I worked in the Ivory Coast. I know your president.'

All bums know all the African presidents. Why doesn't he introduce me to the Canadian prime minister? I haven't even been introduced to the local crime lord!

I sit down on a park pench with the book I started last night. Written by a certain Limonov. A Russian dissident. The 'different dissident' approach. Instead of wasting his time playing the prophet of doom, Limonov gets off with the blacks in Harlem. His book is called *The Russian Poet Prefers Big Blacks*. It begs a rebuttal: *The Black Poet Dreams of Buggering an old Stalinist on the Nevsky Prospect*. New Frontiers Publications.

The Iron Curtain seen as a giant chastity belt.

Bouba came back from the SAVI, a kind of emergency centre for migrants and immigrants. You practically have to provide a complete c.v. and a certificate of good conduct and safe morals before they'll slip you twenty dollars. The working class has had its troubles since the dawn of the industrial revolution. Bouba sold himself today; tomorrow will be my turn. He came back and bought food at Pellatt's. The usual fare: potatoes, rice and chicken (the neck only).

The Black Penis and
the Demoralization of the
Western World

Place des Arts subway. The 80 bus, north. Get off at Laurier and Park. Bar Isaza. Steep stairway. Smoky landscape. Waves of black gold moving across the dance floor. Starched dashikis. Negroes in rut. A few dozen white mice come to play in the lair of the Black Cat.

'There they are.'

'Where?'

'At the back, to the right.'

'Okay, Bouba. I'm going to have a piss first.'

Men's john. Two jet-black Negroes.

NEGRO ONE: You have to be quick with these girls, brother, or they'll slip through your fingers.

NEGRO TWO: That's the way it is!

NEGRO ONE: They came here to see black. We've got to show them black.

NEGRO TWO: What's this black business?

NEGRO ONE: Listen, brother, cut the innocence. You're here to fuck, right? You're here to fuck a white woman, right? That's how it works.

NEGRO TWO: But a woman can be....

NEGRO ONE: There's no women here. There's black and white – that's all!

Streaming bodies. Eighteen-carat ebony. Ivory teeth. Reggae music. Combustion. Black fusion. A white / black couple practically copulating on the dance floor. Atomic shockwaves.

Bouba introduces me.

'My brother. We live together.'

The girls smile.

'What do you do?' one of them asks me.

'I write. I'm a writer.'

'Really? What do you write?'

'Fantasies.'

'What kind?'

'Mine.'

'Are they good?'

'We'll see.'

The girl gazes sadly at the dance floor, then asks me what I think about it.

'Nothing – except that black and white are accomplices.'

'Accomplices! Where's the murder?'

'The murder of the white man. Sexually, the white man is dead. Completely demoralized. Look at them dancing. Do you know any white man who could keep up with that madness?'

Hard-core cruise. Savage thrust. A few white guys gesticulating in the corner. Everything else is a black tide, washing over the dance floor, filling the room. Here and there a woman is trapped like a seagull with its feet caught in heavy oil. Brazilian music: slow, insinuating, languorous. The air is sticky. Opaque sensuality.

'Want to dance?'

It's like moving into Amazon humidity. Bodies running with sweat. You need a machete to cut through this jungle of arms, legs, sexes and mingling smells. Spicy sensuality. She presses against me. No talking. The samba flows into our bodies. Sweat pouring down. Everything flowing. Effortlessly. We've got all eternity.

We go back to the table.

'Your business about sexuality,' she declares, 'is a load of crap.'

'If you say so.'

'You're just reworking the Myth of the Black Stud. I don't believe in it.'

'What do you believe in?'

'Black and white are the same to me.'

'We're talking sexuality, not arithmetic.'

'Sure. But....'

'Since you've challenged me, I'm going to tell you exactly what I think. Black and white are equal when it comes to death and sexuality. Eros and Thanatos. And I think that when you mix black man and white woman you get blood red. With his own woman the black man might not be worth the paper he's printed on, but with a white woman, the chances of something happening are good. Why? Because sexuality is based on fantasy and the black man / white woman fantasy is one of the most explosive ones around.'

'Emotions are black – isn't that myth a little worn out?'

'It might be. But you can't have whites winning coming and going. They say they're better than blacks in everything, then turn around and want to be our equals in one area: sexuality.'

'What about whites who don't think they're superior to blacks?'

'Those whites, obviously, don't have sexual hang-ups.'

A meringue.

'Let's give it a try.'

Koko, the Senegalese musician I met at the Clochards Célèstes, has a hot tip for me.

'This girl at my table is suffering an attack of the mystical heebie-jeebies over you.'

'Why would that be, brother?'

'She insists you're the reincarnation of the Great God Râ.'

'As if I needed that.'

'If you want you can stop by my table.'

I let a couple minutes go by, then go over to where Koko is sitting.

'Hi, Koko.'

'Hi, brother. Sit down.'

The girl is as cool and composed as a pressure cooker.

'How are you doing?'

'Not bad.'

The DJ is playing reggae.

'You want to dance?'

'Okay.'

Brazilian music comes on.

'Should we stay?'

'Fine with me.'

It's that easy when it's working. Smooth as silk.

'Let's get a drink at the bar,' she says. 'It's quieter there. We can talk.'

We sit down at the bar on the high stools and order drinks. I ask her what she's up to these days.

'I'm reading.'

'What?'

'Hemingway.'

'Excellent.'

We finish our drinks. She asks me back to her place for coffee.

'I'll come.'

'Are you leaving with that girl?' Bouba asks me as I get my jacket from the back of the chair.

'Looks that way.'

'The girl next to me says you dropped her because she didn't agree with everything you said.'

'Tell her, Bouba, that all I did was beat her to the punch.'

'Looked to me she was hot for you. She told me it was the first time anyone's ever put her down.'

'Tell her that times are tough for everybody.'

I wish them all a good night. The girl with Bouba, Miz Zodiac, smiles back. Miz Mystic too. A put-on smile. The other girl was waiting for me at the door.

The Black Cat with Nine Tails

She lives in Notre-Dame-de-Grâce, all the way across town. A nice place. Across from a park. Another girl across from a park. But this park has nothing in common with the Carré St. Louis. She cohabits with two cats: Lady Barbarella of Odessa and Blue Salvador Nasseau, otherwise known as Mitzy.

Lady Barbarella is the playful, mischievous, romper-room type. Sir Nasseau the grumpy one. It's obvious that the apartment belongs to them.

'A drink?'

'Daquiri, please.'

Miz Cat moves into the kitchen and I hear her rinsing the glasses in the sink. She adds the ice cubes. I try to interpret every movement.

The room is divided into two unequal halves by a black oilcloth. The smallest half, probably the bedroom, has a yellow sofa and a tiny set of shelves which contain erotica only: J. J. Pauvert's celebrated collection, Miller's complete works (*Nexus, Sexus, Plexus*), *The Story of O*, the publications of Régine Desforges, Lucien de Samosate's *Oeuvre amoureuse*, Aretini, Rachilde and Octave Mirabeau. The other side of the screen, more spacious, is less impressive. Prints, a wicker chair, a few cushions and photographs of cats all over the walls. Famous cats. Literary cats. Art critical cats. Communist cats. Aristocats. Vegetarian cats. Lustrée and Fourrure, Malraux's cats when he lived in Buisson-les-Verrières. Bébert, Céline's cat. Léautaud's pussy. Remy de Gourmont's cat. Huxley's cat and Claude Roy's cat. Cocteau's feline. Colette's creamy female. Carson McCullers' stray cat and a few photos of Lady Barbarella in Cuba, Mexico (gazing at the ruins of an Aztec temple), Trinidad, London, China (walking on the Wall) and Singapore.

Miz Cat is still working on my daquiri in the kitchen. It is always hard to begin a normal conversation with a person you've just met, more or less a chance encounter. Besides, when we're talking black man and white woman, who are already separated by light-years of metaphysical distance, the slightest physical distance increases the difficulty considerably. In these circumstances of separation – she in the kitchen, I in the living room – the conversation drifted (Allah knows why) onto the topic of famine and cats.

'What?'

'I said that....'

'I can't hear you.'

'I was saying....'

'Talk louder.'

'In my country, people eat cats!'

This time, of course, she heard. At that precise moment I realized I had just committed the gaffe of the century.

'I don't, of course,' I added as quickly as I could.

Too late. What's done is done. She brought me my drink with a constipated look on her face, and bravely we tried to change the subject.

'I bet you like to read a lot.'

'I do. I spend a fortune on books.'

She glances at her library. Maybe she's forgotten the incident. What man could love books on one hand, and on the other hand eat cats? I could have told her I appreciated the savour of human flesh, not as gamey as I like, of course, but a pinch of salt helps it go down. I could have told her that and she wouldn't have blinked. A guy who eats human flesh isn't necessarily any worse than anyone else.

But cats are another matter. Deep down, she's right. Everyone loves a lover. Now she's smiling sweetly at me. The alert has been called off. Suddenly I feel an irresistible urge to piss. The third door to the right. I empty my bladder. Whew! I consider my reflection in the mirror. The Montreal Cat-Strangler. I don't look the part, but you can't judge a book.... What got into me to reveal such an intimate thing? The Devil made me do it. Beelzebub. The Spirit of the Bush that trips up the Negro every time he tries to scale the Judeo-Christian ladder. Perhaps it was a sign from Allah. To avoid compromising myself with this infidel. ('Speak of what has been revealed to you in the Book, obey the necessity of prayer, for prayer preserves you from the impurity of sin and all blameful actions. To keep Allah in your heart is your duty. Allah knows your actions.') Why did I say, 'In my country, people eat cats'? What made me pronounce such words? Fortunately, she does not seem too upset. But why do it in the first place? I splash my face vigorously. White teeth, fire in my eyes. Sexy. Ready for the war between the sexes. I emerge.

And see Miz Cat in the hall, panicky, holding Lady Barbarella of Odessa and the phlegmatic Sir Blue Salvador Nasseau in her arms.

If I don't waste too much time in needless apology, I might still be able to catch the last subway at one-thirty.

The West Has Stopped Caring about Sex, That's Why It Tries to Debase It

I wake up to the notes of *Saxophone Colossus*. Bouba is saying his first prayer of the day. Clean dishes, peonies next to my Remington. Manna in the fridge: cheese, pâtés, milk, eggs, yogurt, fresh vegetables. Miz Literature visited us as we slept. She left a note by the typewriter.

Dear Man, Are you still among the living? If so, let me know. If not, go to hell.
    I offer you three choices:

1. Come by at noon and we'll eat at the McGill cafeteria.
2. Come by this afternoon if you know how to play badminton and meet me in the gym.
3. Tonight Braxton is at the Rising Sun. Me too. – L.

I fix a quick but copious meal. The sun still uncertain. The Remington, always faithful, with its blank page stuck down its throat. Bouba winds up his prayer. ('We spread the heavens like a canopy and provided it with strong support: yet of its signs they are heedless.' Sura XXI, 33.)

I sit down in front of the typewriter. Bouba is having his breakfast.

'Did it work out all right last night, Bouba?'

'She's totally crazy, man.'

'That's the way you like them, I thought.'

'Not all the time, man. She wanted to do my astrological chart. Fuck the stars. She took me to her place on Park Avenue. A five-and-a-half, worse than the Oratory. Dark. Mystical bookshelves. Big blow-ups of the maharaji. Every crazy-man was hanging on her wall. She's totally out to lunch. We sit down lotus-style on reed mats. She tucks her legs under her mystic ass. Legs that would drive the most ascetic bunch of Buddhist monks wild. We do a little meditation. My soldier is standing up straight.'

'What's she doing?'

'Absolutely nothing. I got up and took a piss to show her that a human being, even a black one (especially a black one!) is made of flesh and blood, muscle and piss. She didn't move. She uncoiled her legs and went into her room and came out with the tools of her trade. She wanted to do my chart at two o'clock in the morning. Date of birth, place, time, the whole thing: Jupiter influences Saturn and Saturn influences me, and I couldn't influence her. Finally she remembered I was there. She got up to run a bath. I like a nice hot bath, but it really wasn't the moment for it. It did smell good, like leaves. But I'm not the aquatic type. I was on fire. In the water. That kind of combination is hard on a man's nerves. Then she put on a Hindu record, something like *The Sacred Music of Plants of the Far East*. You can listen all you like but you won't hear a thing.

Plant music, man. Plants aren't too talkative. All that was missing was the incense. I'm telling you, brother, the West can't get a hard-on without some kind of stimulant. No natural hard-ons.'

'The Philosopher-King speaks.'

'I'm warming up for my interview. Can you see me on TV, with noted sexologist-for-the-people Janette Bertrand: my opinion, Mme Bertrand, is that we have too many distractions. Leisure time, the bomb, religion, marijuana, TV. Madame, we are the last ones to get off on sex. Whites have lost their interest in it. Though I'm not talking about the women ... some interest is still apparent. Am I shocking your audience?'

'Not at all. On this program we're free to discuss everything. But what about porno films and dirty books; wouldn't you say that that disgusting proliferation proves that whites, despite what you say, are still interested in amorous activity – in sex, as we say in modern language?'

'It's a trap, madame. The West no longer cares about sex; that's why it tries to debase it. It's all directed against blacks because the Judeo-Christian world believes sex is their domain only. It can't help but knock down the merchandise. But we blacks must restore sex to its full glory.'

'Is that the theme of your New Crusade?'

'In so many words.'

Bouba must need a sleep cure if he's confusing a Negro with Janette Bertrand. (Me Tarzan, you Jane.) People have been talking about mutation for a long time now. But I didn't know it had gone that far.

The First Black Vegetarian

Just as I was finishing that chapter, Bouba came in with a fabulous girl. California style. Sun and orange groves. White teeth and sparkling smile. A regular cover girl. Finally! At last!

'Forget the dishes, man, we're eating out.'

'It couldn't come at a better time. I just finished the first draft of my novel.'

'Did you hear that? He just finished it.'

Bouba grabs the manuscript and goes dancing around the table.

'I could use a shower,' I say.

'We'll wait, Homer.'

A shower. A novel on the go. A knock-out girl and a meal in the cards. Some days it all works. I finish my shower. My head is spinning. Allah is taking a personal interest in me these days.

'Are you vegetarians?' Miz Cover Girl asks sweetly.

'No, herbivores.'

She smiles. I know that perfect happiness is not of this world. ('Had they believed in Allah and the Prophet and that which is revealed to him they would not have befriended the unbelievers. But many of them are evil-doers.' Sura V, 81.)

A crummy restaurant on Duluth Street.

Nuts and berries on the menu. A dozen diners religiously munching on bowls of alfalfa. We take a table at the rear, back to the wall. The sound of mouths masticating reminds us of a mosque. We listen to the vegetarian credo mouthed by a herd of cud-chewers. We order our meal from a nature girl who looks as though she was raised in an alfalfa field. Cuisine à la sunflower oil. In the restaurant, twenty-odd wooden tables are scattered through three small rooms. The walls are cluttered with maharaji brochures, eco-agro journals, mystical propaganda and comic strips. How can you eat in this decor? The guests look desperate in their lumberjack shirts. On the wall behind me I read this appetizing offer: 'Christine, organic woman into spiritual ways, seeks to share house in the country. Prepared to share with one or more people who wish to experience forms of Chinese energy (tai chi and acupuncture) in a beautiful natural setting.' Cruising verboten no doubt; too bad, it would be curious to see a Negro performing forms of Chinese energy with a white girl. A large poster displays a tunic-clad young woman: MARGILIS. Margilis at the Conventum. MARGILIS UNLEASHED. We hit the Conventum. In the lobby, we admire an exhibition of caged apes wearing tutus next to six large black-and-white posters of an off-Broadway play. We go in. Margilis. Intermission. I go to the john. A coded message next to the mirror: New York, Luigi? Jojo, Smith. Paris Lucienne Lambale / London Marie Lambert Co. / Principal dancer for Talk of the Town, 'émission zoom / ballet jazz de Montréal Eddy Toussaint & Co.'

I go up to Miz Cover Girl, who's absorbed in conversation with two other girls. She does the introductions. One of the girls is skinny; the other enormous. A biological scandal and an anthropological curiosity. There's Miz Alfalfa (the nice one), nature-girl, clear skin, freckles, smell of hay, probably goes for love in the stables. She emanates a robust sensuality. The other one is a walking skeleton, no breasts (not even a trace), smokes three packs of cigarettes a day and writes poetry. Miz Alfalfa, naturally, tends the alfalfa fields in a commune called 'The Together Revolution Alfalfa Company Inc.' She eats, talks, sells and shits alfalfa. Probably fucks it too. One day she'll give birth to alfalfa babies. While Miz Alfalfa tells us the heroic tale of alfalfa, Miz Gitane is smoking up a storm.

Margilis, part 2. No one wants to make a decision. We go into the Conventum bar and gulp down a merguez sandwich. Next on the menu is a poetry reading at the Dazibao gallery that no one wants to miss. Bouba and I were hoping to stop off at Zorba's for a souvlaki, out of nostalgia for meat.

Dazibao, rue St-Hubert, up above Café Robutel. To get there you have to climb a steep stairway welded to the Robutel like a handle on a coffee cup. The price of admission is a stack of copies of the *NBJ*, the magazine for avant-garde poets. Total cost: $2.50. Whither Mayakovsky and the era of free poetry? Inside, every rejection-slip poet in Montreal. Alcoholic, mystical, lumberjack, truck-driver, tubercular poets and cruised-out poetesses. Bouba and I find room in the rear. A great big guy next to Bouba screams bloody murder after every strophe. Cases of beer at his feet. Poetry by the bottle. An enormous poetess, as round as a beer-barrel, tells the story of her lumberjack lover who was jealous of her books. A gentle giant wanted to sing us a lullaby. Another poetess, totally drunk, sits down between Bouba and me. Then the enormous poetess returns to the stage to tell the story of her lover whose feet stank. Make love with your boots on or get out. Most of the time he did it without his boots and the house stank for a week afterward. I went home. The novel was waiting for me. I put my last beer next to the Remington and made a sandwich. It was going to be a long night.

My Old Remington Kicks Up Its Heels While Whistling Oh Dem Watermelons

Horizon obscured. I can't make out much. I've been in isolation for three days with a case of Molson, three bottles of wine, two cans of Ronzoni spaghetti, five pounds of potatoes and this goddamn Remington. Next to the bell downstairs, I put up a sign that any idiot can understand: 'Do Not Disturb: Great Writer Writing Last Masterpiece.' After three days of straight typing, the lower-case letters are beginning to look iridescent. The capitals resemble those hairy spiders from the tropics. The room pitches lightly on a sea of Molson. Waves of dense heat flow over my back. The consonants fornicate and whelp as I look on. The dishes pile up. The garbage can is overflowing. I'm suffocating. I watch, inert, as the cockroaches go about their business. The room is running in ultramarine humours. How not to consider yourself a genius under such conditions? This horrid heat! I can picture Homer, old Homer himself, typing out his first book, his Iliad, under the Mediterranean sun. Borges would have kept his anthracite suit at 88 degrees F. Bukowski too. Not Saint-John-Perse, despite his Caribbean roots. All you need is a good Remington, no cash and no publisher to believe that the book you're composing with your gut feelings is the masterpiece that will get you out of your hole. Unfortunately, it never works that way. It takes as much guts to do a good book as a bad one. When you have nothing, you can always hope for genius. But genius has refined tastes. It doesn't like the dispossessed. And nothing is all I've got. I'll never make it out of here with a so-so manuscript.

I write by day.
   And dream by night.

In my dream I walk past the Hachette bookstore on St. Catherine Street. I see my novel in the window under an enormous poster: 'A Young Black Montreal Writer Puts James Baldwin out to Pasture.' I go inside. My book is positioned between Moravia and Greene. Good company. That book, holding its own, with that red and yellow cover and jazz look – that book is me. Completely me. I am those 160 tight little pages. Someone is going to come in any moment now, pick up my book and leaf through it, dubious at first then delighted, he's going to go to the cash and give the cashier the $12.95 that will get him the book. The cashier will put my book in a Hachette bag and give it to him. The guy will go home with his new purchase: my book. And this man, miracle of miracles, will be my first real reader.

The bookseller comes up to me. He recognizes me. My picture is on the end papers.
   'Sir....'
   And this man, miracle of miracles, is the first white man to call me sir.

'Excuse me, sir....'

I pretend I didn't hear him. It's such a novelty to my ears. I let it linger there a while.

'Sir....'

'Yes.'

'I read your book.'

'Oh, thank you!'

Oh, how proper I've become!

'It's very powerful.'

'Is it selling?'

Oh, how mercantile I've become!

'It's doing very well.'

'Good.'

'Hasn't anyone told you?'

'I was in New York. I got back last night. I haven't even spoken to my publisher.'

'I see. Come into my office, you can call him from there.'

And I do.

'Hello....'

'Who is this?'

'I don't know if you'll remember me....'

'I don't know either.'

'I sent you a manuscript....'

'We're having a bad season. Very bad. What was our answer?'

'The manuscript was called *Black Cruiser's Paradise.*'

'Where the hell were you? We've been looking for you everywhere.'

'I was there.'

'There where?'

'I was in New York. I always go to New York this time of year.'

'Good for you. Your book is out and it looks like it's doing well.'

'Is it selling?'

'Not so fast....'

'I'm at Hachette.'

'Don't listen to booksellers, they don't know anything about anything. They're just salesmen. They take no risks. None whatsoever.'

'Where's the success, then?'

'The critics, my friend. The critics are bowing down to you.'

'I'm flattered. How much is that worth?'

'Don't use that cynical tone with me, young man. You'll have plenty of opportunity to act cynical with Madame Bombardier.'

'Miz B-52!'

'Not so fast.... You'll be going on Bombardier's show, *Noir sur Blanc*. Fits you like a glove, wouldn't you say? Meanwhile, we'll work on what we have, and what we have is a superb piece by Jean-Ethier Blais.'

'Blais!'

'Himself in person, my friend, in fits of admiration. Get yourself a chair and listen to what Mr. Blais has to say: "I have never read anything so strong, so original, yet so obvious. This is the most horrifying portrait of Montreal I have read in years. If what this young man says is true, then we must conclude that our brand of liberalism is the most incredible hogwash that ever existed (something I've always suspected)." And Pierre Vallières took five columns in *La Presse* to say: "Finally, the true *Black Niggers of America!*"

'Uhh ... that's nice of them.'

'That's nice of them? Is that all you have to say? Don't I get any credit? I know you authors, you write your little books in your dingy basements with delusions of grandeur about being Henry Miller. And when it works one time in a thousand, you act so innocent.... Oh yeah, someone called and asked you to call them back.'

'Carole Laure.'

'How do you know?'

'I just know.'

Carole Laure. Carole Laure. CAROLE LAURE. Carrel Or. What am I going to say to CL? I wrote a book with my guts to get a call from CL. And it worked – she called. What are you supposed to feel at a time like this? I can't feel a thing.

'Hello....'

'Yes, this is Carole Laure.'

'I think you called my publisher.'

'Oh, it's you!'

'I was in New York. My publisher gave me your message today.'

'What are you doing now?'

'What am I doing now??'

'Oh, I understand. Have you eaten yet?'

'Me? No.'

'It's my treat. Where are you now?'

'Me?' I'm not entirely sure. 'I'm at the corner of St. Catherine and Berri.'

'I'm not far. Do you know Prince Arthur Street?'

'Yes.'

'I'll see you soon.'

I've got a date with CL on Prince Arthur. On Prince Arthur ... where on Prince Arthur? Oh, shit! For fucking Allah's sake! I forget to ask her where. I can't start looking for CL in every restaurant on Prince Arthur. I can't stand Carole Laure up!

The literary section of Saturday's *La Presse* is supposed to run an article on me with the headline 'A New Genius.' Some genius! Can't even make a date right.

Cut to Radio-Canada, for the taping of the show *Noir sur Blanc*.

Miz Bombardier looks straight at the camera and the show begins: 'The novel you will be reading this season is called *Black Cruiser's Paradise*. It was written by a young black Montreal writer, and it's his first book. The critics have greeted it with the most enthusiastic praise. Jean-Ethier Blais states that he has read nothing like it in generations. Réginald Martel says the book is the first in a search for new literary forms. Gilles Marcotte has spoken of "a filter of lucidity through which violence and eroticism of the most explicit sort acquire a certain purity." A junior college teacher in Montreal has included it in his course on Racism and Society. David Fennario is currently translating it into English, and plans to adapt it into a play he'll call "Negroville."'

Miz Bombardier turns her attention to me.

'I read your book and I laughed, but it seems to me you don't like women.'

'Negroes too.'

Miz B. smiles. I won the first round.

'But you do go a little far....'

'When people reveal their fantasies, you'll usually find something for everyone – or against everyone. Let me point out that for all intents and purposes there are no women in my novel. There are just types. Black men and white women. On the human level, the black man and the white woman do not exist. Chester Himes said they were American inventions, like the hamburger or the drive-in. In my book, I give a more ... personal version of them.'

'Very personal indeed. I read your novel. It takes place around the Carré St. Louis. In a nutshell, it's the story of two young blacks who spend a hot summer chasing girls and complaining. One loves jazz; the other literature. One sleeps all day or listens to jazz while reciting the Koran; the other writes a novel about their day-to-day experiences.'

'That's it.'

'Let me ask you something.'

'Go right ahead.'

'Is it true?'

'Is what true?'

'Did all those things really happen to you? I ask because, in your real life, you live in the same neighbourhood, off the Carré St. Louis. You live with a friend and you're a writer, like your narrator.'

'Pure coincidence.'

'Perhaps. Your novel is the first portrait of Montreal from the pen of a black writer. Admit that you were a bit harsh.'

'You think so?'

'But your readers like that because they're used to a more plaintive sort of Negro.'

'The ones in my novel never stop complaining.'

'Yes, but the tempo is different. They're tougher, sharper, more pugnacious. They're complainers, but they know how to hit back. Humour is their most effective weapon.'

'That's the way life is. You parry the blows and you strike back.'

'Their weapons are quite different. Generally, blacks appeal to Africa, but your characters never do. Why not?'

'Because they live in the Western world.'

'But they're Moslems!'

'True. Their faith belongs to Islam, but their culture is totally European. Allah is great, but Freud is their prophet.'

'Odd Moslems indeed!'

'The portrait is real. For when a black man and a white woman meet, the lie is the predominant feature.'

'Aren't you painting things a little too black?'

'Last night I was in a bar downtown. A black man and a white woman were sitting next to me. I knew the guy. He was all but telling her he was a cannibal, fresh out of the bush, that his father was the big medicine-man in his village. The whole mythology. I watched the girl: she was nodding, in total ecstasy at finding a real bushman, homo primitivus, the Negro according to *National Geographic*, Rousseau and Company. I know the guy and I know he's not from the bush. He's from Abidjan, one of Africa's great cities. He lived in Denmark and Holland for quite a while before coming to Montreal. He's an urban man, a virtual European. But he'd never admit that to a white girl for all the ivory in the world. In the white man's eyes, he wants to be a Westerner; but with a white woman, Africa serves as his supernumerary sex.'

'What about the girl?'

'She was beside herself. She had found her African. Her primitive.'

'You're a harsh judge of people.'

'A harsh judge for harsh times. Don't forget that the guy was wounded in his way too. Do you know what he told me in the men's room? He asked me, "Do you know why Whites never say that a black is ugly?" I didn't know the answer; he did. "Because, so far, they're not sure of our true nature."'

'Can you elaborate?'

'We never say that a cat is ugly. Either we praise the animal or we keep quiet. We're not entirely sure about animals. We say that the tiger is a handsome animal, but we don't know what the other animals in the jungle think. And we never talk about specific tigers. We say, the tiger. It's the same thing for blacks. People say, the blacks. They're a type. There are no individuals.'

'Aren't you exaggerating a little?'

'I may be.'

'How have blacks reacted to your book?'

'They want to lynch me.'

'Why is that?'

'Because I let the cat out of the bag. They don't like being caught with their pants down. They say I've sold out, that I'm playing the white man's game, that my book is no good and the only reason it was published was because whites need a black man around to carry on and give whites a clear conscience.'

'Is that your opinion?'

'I have no opinion. I make no statements without consulting my lawyer – unless they're about writing. That's not what the Moral Majority thinks. They say my book is the kind of trash that pollutes the reader, whose only goal is to debase the white race by attacking its most sacred object: Woman. You see, I've hit the jackpot.'

'Doesn't that bother you?'

'What? Debasing white women?'

'No. Your black readers' opinion.'

'To be a traitor is every writer's destiny. I hope that's the first cliché in this interview.'

'A final question: are you going to write another book?'

'Yes. Three others. It's in the contract.'

'Good luck.'

The Negroes Are Thirsty

Last night Bouba dragged in a couple of half-dead females. Both
of them were dogs. He'd picked them up on St. Catherine.
Everyone knows no one's ever seduced a girl with an offer of a
place to sleep. They had to be dogs.

When he came in Bouba whispered to me that the big one
was mine and I could do whatever I wanted with her: fuck her,
sell her, throw her out the window. I didn't want any part of it.
It wasn't in my job description. A month ago I would have
considered her manna from heaven. ('On the day when they
behold the scourge with which they are threatened, their life on

earth will seem to them no longer than an hour. That is a warning. Shall any perish except the evil-doers?' Sura XLVI, 35.) But these days I'm on a diet. I've lost my taste for gimps, drunks, poetesses, what-the-cat-dragged-in's, sick of all those girls that nobody will take except bums and blacks. I want a normal girl with a conservative father and a bourgeois mother (both racist to the core), a real live normal girl, not a blow-up doll smashed on beer. Shit, I've got a thirst for a decent life. I am thirsty. The Gods are thirsty. Women are thirsty. Why not Negroes? The Negroes are thirsty.

The Big One was worse than a crushed cockroach on a Sunday night. She didn't even see me; she flung open the fridge door and helped herself to a beer. Big, ugly and vulgar. ('Fighting is obligatory for you, much as you dislike it.' Sura II, 216.) Up above, Beelzebub is lying low. Very low!

Bouba started undressing the Little One and feeling up her breasts. The Big One had had time to put away three beers and still not notice me. I scrunched down in the bed. Bouba signalled me to take care of the Big One and went on feeling up the Little One. I was laying in wait for the Big One behind the eleventh beer. Then the ceiling came tumbling down with a tremendous crash. It had to happen sooner or later. Columns of pink smoke. But we were spared the worst. Escaping death by inches. Beelzebub wasn't lying low up there after all.

The Big One went and stood in the shower with all her clothes on and and started screaming at the top of her lungs. She was hungry. She went and cooked up some spaghetti. Soaking wet. I don't know when I finally snapped. I didn't stop screaming for over an hour. The police came. I fell asleep right afterwards. The next morning the girls were gone.

A grimy noon. Bouba went out. I'm typing the last chapter at top speed. The end of my ordeal is in sight. The Remington (my partner in crime) hasn't lost its touch. I've just got to finish this prologue. When you add it up, I wrote this novel in thirty-six days and eighteen nights, using three ribbons, four jars of liquid paper, five hundred sheets of bond paper, thirty bottles of wine and a dozen cases of beer. I totalled it up in a little black notebook, a gift from Miz Literature. I'm typing like crazy. The Remington is having a ball. Words are squirting out everywhere.

115

I type. I can't take it any more. I type. I'm at the end of my ribbon. I finish. I crash out on the table next to the typewriter with my head on my arms.

You're Not Born Black,
You Get That Way

Dawn came up, as always, independent of my will. Sweet
adolescent dawn. The lances of the sun without their sting.
Gentle and cajoling. My novel stares at me from the table, next
to the old Remington, in its fat red folder. My novel is a
handsome hunk of hope. My only chance. *Take it.*

A NOTE ON THE AUTHOR

Danny Laferrière was born in Port-au-Prince,
Haiti, and worked as a journalist under Duvalier.
In 1978, after a colleague with whom he was
working on a story was found murdered by the
roadside, Laferrière went into exile in Canada. He
now lives in Florida.